"I trusted ⬛⬛⬛⬛⬛⬛⬛⬛⬛⬛⬛ en you made that promise ⬛⬛⬛⬛⬛⬛⬛⬛." Her eyes filled with tears. "I guess ⬛⬛⬛ n idiot, right? I should've known better. I should've guessed you were only spending time with me because"—her voice broke—"you wanted to take my picture for that ridiculous contest."

Jim looked anguished. "Shel, I'm so sorry. I was the idiot, I admit it. But if you'd just let me explain—"

"You promised me that you'd never take a picture of me again and that you'd never show it to anyone if you did." She glared at him. "So what do you do? You enter a picture of me in a contest, hoping that it'll get published. That way the whole world can laugh at me instead of just you and Olivia Davidson!"

Now Jim was starting to get angry, too. "Shelley, you're being ridiculous. No one is laughing at you. The whole reason—"

Shelley cut him off. "Don't you dare call me ridiculous!" she cried. "You're the one who's trying to make me look like a fool by taking a picture of me and plastering it all over the papers! You broke your promise. How can I ever trust you again?" And with that she spun on her heel and ran down the hallway toward the locker room.

Bantam Books in the Sweet Valley High Series
Ask your bookseller for the books you have missed

SWEET VALLEY HIGH

PERFECT SHOT

Written by
Kate William

Created by
FRANCINE PASCAL

BANTAM BOOKS
NEW YORK · TORONTO · LONDON · SYDNEY · AUCKLAND

RL 6, IL age 12 and up

PERFECT SHOT
A Bantam Book / May 1989

Sweet Valley High is a registered trademark of Francine Pascal.

Conceived by Francine Pascal

Produced by Daniel Weiss Associates, Inc.,
27 West 20th Street, New York, NY 10011

Cover art by James Mathewuse

ISBN 0-553-27915-7

Published simultaneously in the United States and Canada

Bantam Books are published by Bantam Books, a division of Bantam Doubleday
Dell Publishing Group, Inc. Its trademark, consisting of the words "Bantam
Books" and the portrayal of a rooster, is Registered in U.S. Patent and Trademark
Office and in other countries. Marca Registrada. Bantam Books, 666 Fifth Avenue,
New York, New York 10103.

PRINTED IN THE UNITED STATES OF AMERICA

O   0 9 8 7 6 5 4 3 2 1

PERFECT
SHOT

One

Elizabeth Wakefield stood in the doorway of Sweet Valley High's crowded lunchroom, anxiously searching for her boyfriend, Jeffrey French.

"There he is. Over there!" Enid Rollins exclaimed, pointing to a corner table.

Enid was Elizabeth's best friend, and right now she was almost as excited as Elizabeth about what Roger Collins, the English teacher, had just told them. The *Sweet Valley News* was sponsoring a photography competition, and both girls wanted to tell Jeffrey about it. Jeffrey was an avid photographer in addition to being an excellent soccer player and one of Sweet Valley High's most handsome juniors.

"Hi!" Jeffrey said, his green eyes lighting up when the girls came over. He squeezed Elizabeth's hand affectionately and then smiled at Enid.

1

"I was hoping you guys would show up." He grimaced at the macaroni and cheese on his plate. "It's barely edible, but I'm starving."

"Jeffrey," Elizabeth began, pulling up a chair, "we were just talking to Mr. Collins, and he told us all about the *News's* photography contest." Her blue-green eyes shone with excitement. "Did he tell your class about it this morning? It sounds like a terrific opportunity. He said he'd give my class all the details this afternoon."

Jeffrey nodded. "Yeah, he told our class this morning. Not only can you win a brand-new video camera, but you also get your photograph published in the *News*!"

Roger Collins, one of the most popular teachers at Sweet Valley High, had told his classes that he would act as a liaison between the newspaper and the students. He would be accepting photo submissions up until a week from Friday.

"You've got to enter it, Jeffrey," Elizabeth said with characteristic exuberance. "I know you'll have an excellent shot at winning. You're such a good photographer!"

"I don't suppose you're at all biased," Jeffrey teased her.

Enid shook her head. "No way. Elizabeth

knows a great photographer when she sees one. Don't tell me you're thinking about not submitting any of your work."

Jeffrey laughed. "Talk about peer pressure," he complained good-humoredly. "Who said anything about not trying? Of course I'll submit something." He grinned at Elizabeth. "As long as my tried-and-true newspaper pal here helps me decide which photograph to send them."

Jeffrey was referring to the fact that Elizabeth was one of the hardest-working staff writers for *The Oracle*, Sweet Valley High's school paper. Jeffrey was a photographer for the paper, and they had gotten to know each other through working together on *The Oracle*.

"But Mr. Collins said the competition is wide open. The judges aren't really looking for anything in particular," she reminded him.

"Yeah, I guess they just want to encourage young photographers," Jeffrey said, taking another bite of macaroni and cheese. "I wouldn't mind winning a video camera. I can think of someone I wouldn't mind taking movies of!" He winked at Elizabeth.

Enid groaned. "If you two start getting romantic, I'm going to have to leave," she teased them. "Hold off for a minute, OK? Do you have any idea what you're going to submit, Jeffrey?"

"I could submit one of the photos I already have. But what I'd like to do," Jeffrey said, "is shoot several rolls of film and see what I can come up with that's different."

He turned to Elizabeth. "Then you can help me select something to submit."

Elizabeth had to smile. She and Jeffrey were so similar. They were both so serious when it came to pursuing anything related to their future careers. She wanted to be a writer one day, and she was working hard at the paper and in English class, trying to learn as much as she could. She knew how devoted Jeffrey was to photography. He spent hours shooting pictures and developing them. Elizabeth was thrilled that he would finally have the chance to show off his good work.

"Hey," Enid said with a smile, nudging her friend. "Here comes your better half."

Elizabeth looked up and saw her twin sister, Jessica, approaching her table. One look at Jessica's face and she could tell her twin wanted something from her.

"Where in the world did Jessica find that outfit?" Enid continued. "No one could possibly get you two mixed up today."

Elizabeth had to laugh. Jessica's brand-new outfit was straight out of the latest issue of *Ingenue* magazine. Jessica was always involved

4

in something new, whether it was a new fashion trend, a new rock group, or a new way to make money. She liked life in the fast lane, and as she often explained to her twin, that meant changing lanes all the time!

Elizabeth was four minutes older than Jessica, but those four minutes were like light-years. In personality she and Jessica were more like identical opposites than identical twins. If Elizabeth said yes to something, Jessica invariably said no. Elizabeth loved school and studying. She liked to spend her free time with a few special friends, like Jeffrey and Enid. She didn't mind the long hours that working on the newspaper required, and she didn't even mind spending a whole evening doing homework. She was also very organized and could always be counted on to head a committee at school.

But Jessica much preferred the social side of school to the academic. Her friends tended to be much wilder than Elizabeth's, more interested in boys, shopping, and the beach. Jessica always wanted to be in the thick of things. As co-captain of the cheerleading squad and a member of Pi Beta Alpha, the school's most exclusive sorority, Jessica could count on a busy social life. And somehow she always managed to know what everyone in Sweet Valley was up to.

Yet however different the twins were in temperament, Jessica and Elizabeth looked so much alike that strangers, and sometimes even friends, confused them. Both had silky, sun-streaked blond hair, sparkling blue-green eyes, and perfect size-six figures, and each even had a small dimple in her left cheek.

"Liz," Jessica gasped. "I completely forgot we're having an extra cheerleading practice today to get ready for the girls' basketball team playoffs, so—"

"So, let me guess. You need the car, right?"

Jessica looked dumbfounded. "How did you know?"

Jeffrey started to laugh. "Must be ESP, Jessica."

Jessica frowned at him. "So, is that OK, Liz?" she asked, turning back to her sister.

Elizabeth nodded. She dug around in her bag for the keys and then handed them to her twin. "Here you go."

A second later Jessica was off like a shot, calling "Thanks!" over her shoulder as she hurried off to another table to join several other cheerleaders.

"Now, if only you could get a picture of that," Elizabeth said, shaking her head. "You'd have to be awfully quick, though."

"You could call it 'Vanishing Act: Jessica Wake-

6

field and the Disappearing Car Keys,' " Enid joked.

"I'll probably have to win the video camera first," Jeffrey commented. "I doubt I could catch Jessica on film without her looking like a blur."

"Sure you could." Elizabeth giggled. "Just tell her it's going to be in the newspaper!"

"Did you hear about Patrick McLean?" Amy Sutton asked. She and Jessica were getting ready for cheerleading practice in the locker room after school. Amy was standing at the mirror, brushing her blond hair for what seemed like the hundredth time.

"Who's Patrick McLean?" Jessica replied.

"He's head of some dance studio that's just about to open in town." Amy almost always knew things before anyone else, partly because her mother worked as a broadcaster on a TV news show and partly because Amy just prided herself on being the first to get new information. "And he's doing a big promotion for the studio, part of which includes free ballroom dance lessons to anyone who wants them in the gym on Wednesdays after school!"

"Ballroom dancing? Here? You mean—waltzing around and doing the tango and stuff?" Jessica couldn't help laughing. "Who's going to want to do *that*?"

"What do you mean?" Amy said indignantly. "I can't wait! Don't you know anything, Jess? All those movie stars in the thirties and forties always knew how to waltz. You can't fall in love and go on big luxurious cruises and be totally romantic unless you know how to waltz. I mean, really."

Jessica still wasn't convinced. "Oh, yeah?" she said. "Well, what guys in this school are going to let themselves get dragged to ballroom dance lessons? Half of them can't even dance to normal music."

Amy carefully applied some eye crayon under her slate-gray eyes. "I'm not worried," she said smugly. "My experience is that if I want a boy to do something, I can usually make sure he'll do it." She gave Jessica an imperious little smile. "Same usually goes for you, Jess. Don't tell me you're slipping."

Jessica made a wry face. But before she could respond, Amy continued. "Besides, don't you remember that there's a big dance coming up? It couldn't be better timing."

Amy was right! The Varsity Club was holding a dance to honor all of the school's athletes who had earned letters in varsity and junior varsity sports. They had even rented a ballroom in a newly completed luxury hotel in downtown Sweet Valley for the occasion.

Jessica imagined herself floating dreamily in the arms of Kurt Campbell, a handsome senior she had decided she liked. Kurt was a varsity football player, which meant he would definitely be attending the dance. Jessica hadn't really dated anyone seriously since her recent breakup with A. J. Morgan, but she was more than ready to get back in circulation. And dance lessons might make her even more attractive to Kurt. "Hey," she said suddenly as she tied the laces to her tennis shoes in double knots. "What's Patrick McLean like? Is he old or young or what? I mean, will it be absolute torture to go to these lessons?"

Amy shrugged. "Who knows? But we'll find out tomorrow."

The cheerleaders' practice lasted longer than usual that afternoon. As Robin Wilson, who shared the position of co-captain with Jessica, had just explained to the members of the squad, now that the girls' basketball team was in the playoffs against Emerson High, both the team and the cheerleaders were going to be getting a lot of publicity. "So we need to do an extra good job," Jessica added solemnly.

"And remember, our schedules are going to be kind of crazy," Robin pointed out. Robin, a pretty brunette with dark, serious eyes, was used to giving the instructions to the group, since her co-captain had a tendency to be forgetful. "We have to be ready to cheer at every game, as long as the team stays in the running. And with the kind of talent we have on the girls' team, that could be all the way to the top!"

Everyone gave one last cheer, signaling the end of practice.

"I guess the team is really counting on Shelley Novak," Jessica said to Amy as they strolled back across the football field to the gym.

"I still say she looks like a beanpole," Amy said derisively.

"She's one of the best players in the state," Jessica argued. "I think she's supposed to get some kind of big award at the Varsity Club dance. She's scored an amazing number of points this season." Shelley was a junior, like Jessica and Amy, but she usually hung around with the other girls on the basketball team, and none of the cheerleaders knew her very well.

"You think she's going to that dance?" Amy looked astonished. "I thought you asked her about it last week, and she said she wasn't. Who's she going to find to go with her?" Amy asked, referring to a conversation that had taken place the week before. At Amy's bidding, Jessica had asked Shelley if she was planning to go to the dance. Shelley had looked embarrassed and shyly said no.

Jessica shrugged. "She may not have been planning to go before, but now that she's getting this award, she pretty much has to. Besides, I'm sure she can find a date," she added. "She's really pretty."

Amy laughed. "Maybe she is, but she's about six inches taller than most of the guys we know! What guy wants to dance with a girl who's taller than he is? No one *I* know."

Jessica couldn't believe Amy sometimes. Much as she thought her friend was a lot of fun, Amy occasionally surprised her with her mean streak. "I think you have to be tall to play basketball so well," Jessica said. "If we've got a chance this season, it's because of Shelley."

Amy wrinkled her nose. "I don't think basketball is very feminine. I'm glad I'm a cheerleader instead."

Jessica shook her head. "I'm glad the girls on the team don't feel that way, or we wouldn't have anyone to cheer for." She laughed. "The boys' team didn't even qualify for the playoffs this year."

Amy shrugged. "Since when are you such a

girls' sports fan? All I'm saying is that I can't imagine Shelley being very graceful on the dance floor. You don't have to make an issue out of it!"

Jessica didn't respond. They had reached the locker room now, and she stopped for a minute, watching as the girls' basketball team came running in from practice on court.

Shelley was the first person she saw, and Jessica couldn't help disagreeing with Amy's assessment as she watched Shelley run toward them.

True, Shelley was tall, but she had an athlete's toned body. She was beautifully proportioned, and she had long slender legs. In fact, her body was a lot like those of the fashion models Jessica admired in *Ingenue*.

Shelley had coppery, curly hair and beautiful almond-shaped brown eyes. With the right makeup and clothes, Jessica thought she could be striking. And there was no denying how smoothly she moved, both on the court and off.

But Amy had apparently gotten a different impression of the basketball star. "See?" she whispered triumphantly to Jessica. "She'd have to get her date a pair of elevator shoes. Either that or dance with him on her knees." She giggled, and after a minute Jessica broke down and giggled, too.

She still thought Amy was wrong, but she couldn't help laughing at her friend's sense of humor, even if it was a little warped.

And anyway, Jessica was too busy thinking about Kurt Campbell and the upcoming dance lessons to worry about Shelley Novak any longer. If she could waltz into the ballroom looking fantastic, there was no telling what would happen between her and Kurt.

Two

"Hey," Cathy Ulrich said, rattling on the shower curtain. "Didn't you hear me ask for the shampoo?"

"Sorry," Shelley said. She passed Cathy a tube of shampoo and turned off the water, then wrapped herself in a fluffy white towel.

"Something's bugging you, I can tell," Cathy said when she got out of the shower a few minutes later and caught up with Shelley at her locker. "You want to talk about it? You've seemed keyed up all day. Even in practice."

Shelley was drying her hair vigorously with the towel. "It's nothing," she muttered. "I was just—" She glanced at herself in the mirror and bit her lip. "Cath, are you planning on asking anyone to the Varsity Club dance?"

Cathy opened her locker and took out a bottle of body lotion. "I'm not sure," she said matter-of-factly. Cathy's boyfriend, Tim, was a freshman at UCLA, and the two of them saw each other only on occasional weekends and holidays. "I don't think Tim can make it, so I'd have to dredge up a date." She laughed. "And I do mean dredge. I can't think of a single guy I'd want to ask. What about you?"

Shelley looked at her reflection in the mirror and frowned. "I ought to do something about my hair," she said critically, running her fingers through her curls. "It looks so—" She grimaced. "I don't know, so *practical*."

Cathy looked closely at her. "Mmm," she said thoughtfully. "First she wants to know if I'm planning on asking someone to the Varsity Club dance. Then she just happens to start picking on herself with that I-wonder-if-he-thinks-I'm-pretty kind of expression in her eyes." She grinned. "I don't suppose it's possible that *you* might be thinking about the dance yourself, is it?" She took her clothes out of her locker and began to get dressed.

Shelley pretended to concentrate on an almost-invisible mark on her cotton sweater. "Maybe."

"Hey," Cathy chided her. "We've got a lot of big stuff coming up, Shel. Like, we happen to be in the playoffs, and we happen to need to stick together and give each other lots of moral support. So don't you think you'd better unburden yourself to your very best friend and tell me what gives?" She paused for a moment. "It's Greg, isn't it?"

Shelley slumped down on the bench next to her locker and rested her chin on her hands. "I can't stand it," she moaned. "Is this really what it's supposed to feel like when you fall in love? Cathy, I'm a total wreck. All I can do anymore is think about Greg. I know this is corny, but my stomach really does feel like it's got butterflies in it. I can't eat, I can't sleep—" She looked fearfully around to make sure the coach wasn't within earshot. "I can't even keep my mind on basketball anymore!"

"Wow," Cathy said sympathetically, patting her on the shoulder. "You've got it bad, kiddo." She sat down on the bench next to her friend. "Tell me what's up. Does he have any idea how you feel?"

"No," Shelley admitted. "That's the worst part. You know how Greg is. He's the world's most confident guy. He's friendly with everyone, but he still treats me exactly like the girl next door."

"Which is what you are," Cathy reminded her.

Shelley had to smile. It was true. Her family had lived next door to the Hilliards ever since they had moved to Sweet Valley. Greg was a year older than Shelley, and they had grown up together, with Greg acting as her older brother. Greg had two brothers himself, but Shelley was an only child, and she had spent a lot of time with the Hilliard boys when she was little.

In fact, Greg was the one who had first taught her how to shoot baskets. The Hilliards had a basketball hoop set up above their garage door, and by the time she was five, Shelley was shooting baskets every night after dinner with Greg and his brothers. By the time she was in middle school, Shelley was good enough to be on the team. By high school she was a star.

For a long time Greg had been her most supportive fan, coaching her, giving her tips, talking endlessly with her about their favorite players in the NBA, accompanying her to Lakers' games with their dads. Greg's father worked in the same consulting firm as Shelley's father, and the Hilliards and Novaks liked to socialize.

Shelley wasn't sure when things had begun to change. Probably when Greg had started going out with Carol Stern, a pretty girl who was in the senior class with him. At first Shelley had assumed it was natural that she felt bad about Greg falling in love. It made sense. Obviously she and Greg couldn't be as close now that he had a girlfriend.

But six weeks ago Greg and Carol had broken up. Greg told Shelley about it one day while they were walking home from school, and Shelley was astonished to discover her heartbeat speeding up. All of a sudden she didn't feel comfortable around Greg. She didn't feel like horsing around or joking about the Lakers. She blushed every time he looked at her, and she felt tongue-tied and miserable.

Now that she knew he and Carol had broken up, she felt free to admit to herself that her own feelings for Greg were more than just friendly. She had a crush on Greg, a giant-sized crush. And it was beginning to get out of control.

"He'll never like me," Shelley said miserably. She stood up and kicked her locker shut. "Look at Carol. She's one of those tiny, adorable little things—totally uninterested in sports, probably has pink ruffles all over her bedroom. Greg probably thinks I'm an oversize clod." She glared at herself in the mirror. "Look at me. If only I could be normal like everyone else!" She hunched her shoulders to get a better look at her face in the mirror. "I can't even see the top of my head in the mirror, that's how tall I am!"

Cathy laughed. "Yeah. You and half the top fashion models in the world can all mourn together." She collected her workout clothes and put them in her duffel bag. "Anyway, I thought you said Greg and Carol broke up. He couldn't have been too thrilled with her, tiny and ruffled as she is, if they broke up. So why don't you just go for it? Ask him to the dance. The worst thing that can happen is that he says no."

Shelley stared at her, stricken with panic over the whole issue of the dance. "Right. The very worst thing," she repeated.

Sometimes she couldn't believe how unsympathetic Cathy could be. Her very best friend didn't understand that she would rather die than risk asking Greg and having him reject her. Suppose she told him how she felt about him and he laughed at her—what then? She'd never live it down. He and his two brothers would all laugh at her. And so would the whole school when they found out about it.

"Speaking of dancing, I think I'm going to sign up for those ballroom dance lessons," Shelley said. "Maybe if someone could help me move a little more smoothly off the basketball court . . ." She shook her head. "I just don't feel ready to confront Greg yet," she added, then gave Cathy a stern look, indicating that the discussion was over. It was bad enough

19

having to think about Greg Hilliard all the time. She wasn't going to make it worse by talking about him, too!

That afternoon Shelley walked home from practice slowly, deep in thought. She was two blocks away from her house when she saw Greg speed past her on his black racing bike.

"Hey, Shel!" he called, putting on the brakes. He got off his bike and waited for her to catch up with him. When she did, he removed his helmet and started walking the bike beside her. "Congratulations on making the playoffs. Are you psyched for the game on Saturday?"

Shelley nodded, her heartbeat speeding up as Greg looked at her. She couldn't stop thinking how good-looking he was. He was well built for someone so slender and had thick dark brown hair, and eyes that were a beautiful shade of gray. He was tall, although an inch or two shorter than she was.

The whole way back home he talked to her about the basketball playoffs. Ordinarily Shelley would have loved to discuss Emerson's chances, their best players, the team's strategy. But today she wished that just once they could talk about something besides basketball. Something like . . . the dance. Shelley tried to imagine Greg noticing how pretty she looked or making a comment about her appearance. But, no, the playoffs were coming up, and the only interest Greg had in her was as a fellow basketball player. *As always*, Shelley thought. *He treats me like he treats his younger brothers*.

"Hey, I'll see you later," he said when they reached her driveway. "Take it easy, champ." He leaned over and rapped her lightly on the shoulder with his helmet, then got back on his bike and zoomed off.

He called me champ, Shelley thought to herself, her face crimson with embarrassment. *As if I'm a prizefighter or something!* She fumed and walked in the back door of her house, her shoulders slumped. What was the use of trying? Greg would never consider going out with her, not in a million, trillion years.

And how could she blame him? *Look at yourself*, Shelley commanded herself, glancing at the mirror in the mudroom. Six feet of totally undistinguished, overtall human being. Thin, not slender. Gangly, not elegant. Hair curly and "convenient" for sports, not sleek and pretty. *Everything about me is wrong*, Shelley despaired. She plodded into the kitchen, where her mother was busy making a salad for dinner, and dropped into the nearest chair.

"Hi, sweetie. How was your day?" her mother asked brightly.

"Lousy. Mom, why couldn't I have inherited *your* genes instead of Dad's? People on your side of the family aren't giants. You're normal height and so's Nana. Why did I have to turn out to be such a freak?"

Mrs. Novak laughed. "You happen to be very lucky, Shel. I'd give anything to be your height. You're a beautiful, graceful girl, and your height happens to be an asset in your favorite sport, too." She picked up the salad server and began to toss the lettuce. "Wouldn't it be terrible if you were too short to play on the team?"

Shelley scowled. "Believe me, I'd manage. Cathy's five feet nine, and she's one of the best guards in the state. Besides, think of all the things you can't do, being my height," she complained.

Mrs. Novak was familiar with Shelley's self-consciousness about her height, and she always tried to understand just what her daughter was feeling. "Like what, honey? What is it you want to do that you can't do?" she asked.

"Well, take dancing, for instance. I'm an incredible klutz. I can't even walk gracefully, let alone dance!" Shelley cried. "The only place I don't make a total fool of myself is on the bas-

ketball court. Everywhere else I just stick out,
like a giraffe."

"Sweetheart, you're just self-conscious. That's
the worst part of being a teenager—you think
everyone's staring at you," her mother said
soothingly. "Just wait a couple of years. When
you get to college and the guys have had their
growth spurts . . ."

Shelley rolled her eyes. She'd been hearing
the same thing for years: "Just wait till the guys
get taller." What good did that do her now? For
as long as Shelley could remember, she had
been the tallest girl in her class. Every time they
had to line up in order of height, everyone
called out her name to go first and laughed.
And the boys seemed permanently stuck at the
same height: shorter than she was.

"You'll see," her mother was saying. "You're
going to find yourself very glad that you're a
few inches taller than other girls. You've got
such beautiful long legs, and you've got the
kind of build that clothes are made for." She
smiled warmly at her daughter. "Now, tell me
all about today's practice. Are you excited about
the game on Saturday? Mrs. Lilliard was telling
me that you girls are getting all kinds of media
coverage—apparently there'll be reporters from
the *News* and a camera crew from Channel 5
there!"

Shelley couldn't answer right away. She knew how excited her parents were about the basketball playoffs. But she just couldn't bring herself to share what they were feeling. Shelley had always loved the sport, but lately it was beginning to seem to her like another symbol of being different, of standing apart. OK, so she was a good player. Maybe even a great player. She had a chance at being all-state, and she knew she ought to be thrilled. But Shelley couldn't help wondering if the only reason she scored so many points was because she was the tallest girl on the team!

"Mom, I'm going upstairs. I'm pretty tired," she told her mother, keeping her real feelings inside. Shelley knew how upset her mother got when she went on and on about her looks, even though her mother tried to be sympathetic.

Shelley jogged upstairs to her room, kicked off her sneakers, and flung herself down on her bed.

She looked at her sneakers with loathing. How could she possibly expect to dance well when her feet were twice as big as most girls' her age?

She squeezed her eyes shut, trying to imagine herself in a beautiful dress with her hair done perfectly for the big dance. After she received her award, Greg would walk up to her and ask her to dance. Instead of calling her champ, he would call her Shelley, and together they would float across the dance floor, the perfect couple, arms wrapped around each other—and she wouldn't miss a step. They would look into each other's eyes, and she would see he felt the same way she did: ecstatic to be with her and madly in love.

Three

"This is going to be great," Amy whispered to Jessica in the gym Wednesday afternoon as they waited for Patrick McLean to arrive and the first ballroom dance lesson to begin.

"Not a real big turnout," Jessica said dryly. Only a handful of students had shown up, and most of them were girls, Jessica noted with disappointment. She was surprised to see Shelley Novak among them. Elizabeth was there with Jeffrey, and the only other boys there were Winston Egbert, self-proclaimed clown of the junior class; Bruce Patman, the richest and most arrogant boy in the whole school; Jim Roberts, who Jessica knew only by name; and a few seniors, including Greg Hilliard, who was with his old girlfriend, Carol.

"We need more guys," Jessica complained.

26

"Guys with names like Kurt Campbell, right?" Amy joked.

Jessica flipped her hair back over her shoulder. She was about to come up with a retort when the door to the gym opened and the most handsome man she had ever seen in her life walked in.

"Omigod," Amy said, grabbing Jessica's arm. "Don't tell me that's—"

"Hi," the young man said cheerfully, setting a tape player up in the front of the room. "My name's Patrick McLean." He surveyed the group with a friendly smile. "Not that many people interested in learning to dance, huh? Well, maybe we'll get some more people interested by the time we're through."

Amy was pretending to swoon. "I'm going to faint," she told Jessica. "Hold me up."

Jessica couldn't speak. All thoughts of Kurt Campbell had flown right out of her head. "Amy," she said softly, "if I ever told you I was in love before, I was lying. This is it. I'm going to follow that man around till the day I die!"

"Oh, no, you won't," Amy whispered. "Whose idea was it to take lessons from him, anyway? *I'm* the one who's in love with him." She glared at Jessica. And as if to prove that she could get Patrick's attention before Jessica, she spoke up right away. "I bet I could get some more people interested in taking lessons," she cooed loudly, in one of the most flirtatious voices Jessica had ever heard.

Jessica was ready to kill her, but luckily Patrick didn't seem overly excited by Amy's promise. "Well, there's no point forcing people," he said calmly, plugging the tape player into an outlet.

Jessica was trying to guess how old he was. He was really tall—at least six feet three, she thought—with light wavy hair, chiseled features, and penetrating dark eyes. With his slender build and European-style clothes, he looked like a model. Everything about Patrick was cool, down to the tiny diamond stud he wore in his left ear.

Luckily Jessica didn't have to rely on guesswork for his age because Patrick began class by telling them all about himself. "I'm graduating this semester from UCLA, and I'm majoring in dance and theater," he said. "My hope is to start a series of dance studios in Southern California, and the first one I'm opening is going to be in Sweet Valley." He winked at them, and Jessica's heart beat faster. "So I'm hoping to get all of you to fall in love with ballroom dancing and tell your families and friends. That way McLean Studios will really get off the ground."

Everyone smiled and murmured appreciatively

28

—all but Amy, who whispered loudly to Jessica, "I'm in love all right!"

Jessica stared murderously at her and said nothing. If she was going to have to fight for Patrick, she was ready!

Patrick popped a tape into the player and turned to the assembled group. "Now," he said, looking them all over. "I need a partner so I can show you all how to do the box step. The box step is the building block we're going to use for a number of other dances, so you'll need to learn it well." His gaze landed on Shelley Novak. "You—what's your name?"

"Uh, Shelley," she stammered.

Patrick held out his hand to her and smiled. "OK, Shelley, please come up front, give me your hand, and we'll show them a thing or two. Now, watch me, everybody. This is the position you want to assume when you begin. Guys, notice the place where I'm putting my hand on Shelley's back."

Amy nudged Jessica. "That," she whispered, "is going to be me."

"Shut *up*," Jessica said, exasperated.

Patrick demonstrated how to hold a partner's hand, how the neck and head should be aligned, how much space there should be between the partners.

"When I get him in my arms, there isn't

going to *be* any space," Amy continued in a rapturous whisper.

Jessica covered her ears with her hands. She was really glad when the music started and Patrick slowly began demonstrating the box step, with Shelley as his partner.

She couldn't bear hearing Amy make such an idiot of herself. Jessica wasn't going to be a total baby about Patrick like Amy was being. This wasn't just a silly crush, it was the beginning of a serious relationship. And Jessica had every intention of making as big an impression on Patrick as he had made on her.

"Now," Patrick said, turning to face them with a smile when the music ended. "Did everyone understand that?"

Jessica was racking her brains, trying to think of what to say, when Amy spoke up. "Uh, I didn't really get it," she said sweetly, staring up at him and batting her eyelids. "Do you think you could show me?"

"Sure," Patrick said with a good-natured smile. "Thanks, Shelley. You were a great partner." As Shelley moved back toward the assembled group of dancers, Patrick held out his hand to Amy. When he put his hand on her back, Amy threw Jessica a look that said, "OK, he's mine now, so stay away!"

But Jessica wasn't about to let Amy get away

with such a rotten trick. She just waited for the music to end before letting Patrick know that *she* hadn't quite gotten the hang of the box step, either.

Patrick looked a little puzzled. "Generally people catch on right away," he said, looking at Jessica with concern.

Amy could barely hide her delight. "That's right, Jess. Couldn't you figure it out after watching it twice?" she demanded in a very loud stage whisper.

"Let's just move on to the next step and see how it goes," Patrick said, turning back to adjust his tape player. Jessica felt her face turn scarlet, but she wasn't going to show Amy how upset she was.

She would have to plot her revenge very carefully. But she would get it, all right. There was no way she was going to let Amy have Patrick McLean. He was hers!

Shelley was ready to die of embarrassment. What a disaster! First of all, when she had returned to the gym after her shower, who had she run into but Greg and Carol. Greg—and Carol! What were they doing together? She thought they had broken up! Greg had acted awfully cool toward her, too, which probably meant he was trying to impress Carol. Before Shelley could even begin to try to figure out whether or not they were getting back together, the dance teacher had dragged her in front of everyone to dance with him.

Actually, if Greg and Carol hadn't been there looking on, it might have been kind of nice dancing with Patrick. He was the right height, for once, and he was very handsome. And he was so sure of himself and so absolutely in control that she couldn't help moving correctly when he was leading. However, she still couldn't relax, no matter how well they were dancing together. She felt about as stiff as a six-foot ladder, which was probably what she looked like. When the song was over, Patrick stepped back, bowed politely, and turned to the rest of the class.

For the next few minutes, Shelley was so deep in thought that she barely paid attention to what was going on around her. But she was jolted back to the present when Patrick said, "Now, I want everyone to pair up. It doesn't have to be boy-girl, just grab someone and do the steps that we just did."

Shelley stared at Greg, trying to will him to look at her. But he was too busy looking at Carol.

Shelley bit her lip, partly from nervousness

and partly from frustration. She had sworn to herself, and to Cathy, that she was going to broach the subject of the Varsity Club dance with Greg that afternoon, the first chance she got. Why wouldn't he look at her? *Greg,* she thought, trying to send him a telepathic message. *Greg, come over and do the box step with me and quit staring at Carol.*

Her reverie was suddenly interrupted when a boy she didn't know tapped her on the arm. "Uh—do you want to do this box step with me?"

Shelley stared blankly at his unfamiliar face. Surprisingly it was the same height as her own. He had green eyes and sandy hair, and he was OK-looking. Nothing special, though. He seemed very shy.

"My name's Jim Roberts. I've watched you play basketball a lot. I think you're great," he told her.

Shelley looked over at Greg, who was taking Carol's hand. She sighed deeply as she turned back to Jim. "Thanks," she said. She noticed Jim's hand was a little sweaty. He stepped hard on her foot when they tried to assume the starting position, and Shelley winced.

Patrick turned on the music, and the couples started dancing. Shelley looked around the gym, trying to see how everyone else was doing.

Elizabeth Wakefield and Jeffrey French seemed like old pros. Elizabeth's sister, Jessica, on the other hand, was suffering through Winston Egbert's agonizing attempts to turn the box step into a combination of dirty dancing and disco. Amy Sutton had been paired up with Bruce Patman, but she was gazing at Patrick, who was walking back and forth, observing the class. From time to time he called out something like "Nice work!" or "Watch that position!"

Shelley wished the tape player would break. Jim seemed like a nice guy, but he was making her feel like the biggest klutz in the room. To top it all off, he apologized every time *she* stepped on him, as if it were his fault! After their second attempt to form a box failed miserably, Jim seemed as unhappy as Shelley felt.

"I guess I'm not very good at this, huh?" he said when the music stopped and they broke apart. Patrick announced that the class was over and would meet again the following Wednesday.

"No, *you* did fine," Shelley insisted. "I'm the one who—" She broke off mid-sentence and stared at Greg. Carol had grabbed her jacket from the bleachers, and she was wriggling into it. She whispered something to Greg and then headed for the exit by herself. Shelley didn't know whether to be relieved or anxious. With Carol gone, she didn't have any excuse not to discuss the dance with Greg.

Greg turned around and seemed to notice Shelley was in the gym for the first time. "Hey, Novak!" he called out, coming over to her and giving her a playful shove. "Let's walk home together, OK?"

Shelley managed a smile, but her mouth was dry with nervousness. This was it. She was going to find out how Greg felt, like it or not.

"That was fun," Shelley said as she and Greg stepped out the front door of the school.

"Yeah, I guess. I don't know how big I am on that kind of dancing, though." Greg gave an exaggerated yawn, and Shelley giggled. "Carol was really into it, and she asked me to come."

Shelley hesitated. "I thought you two—well, you know . . ."

Greg sighed. "I wish I could figure out what's going on in that girl's head." For a minute he sounded really sad. Then he said firmly, "No, we're broken up for good. I guess Carol still wants to be friends, but that's it."

Shelley was relieved. She shot a quick glance at Greg, who looked thoughtful. "Do you really miss her?" she asked, immediately wishing she could take the question back. She didn't want to know.

"Sometimes." Greg shrugged. He grinned and

leaned over to jab her in the arm. "Let's talk about something more interesting: basketball. You ready for the game on Saturday? Do you think Emerson's got a chance against you?"

Shelley took a deep breath. She wasn't going to let the conversation turn into a sports newscast this time. She had psyched herself up for this conversation as if it were the championship game. Only her relationship with Greg was on the line, not the league title. "Greg," she said boldly, "weren't you surprised to see me show up at that dance class?"

Greg thought it over for a second. "No. Why should I be? I thought girls always liked stuff like that."

"Well, I just want to learn to waltz before the Varsity Club dance," she said, looking at him meaningfully.

"Oh," Greg said, apparently not getting the hint.

But Shelley wouldn't give up. "You know about that dance, right? It's going to be held at that new hotel downtown, two weeks from Friday."

"Yeah," Greg said. "I got an invitation from the Varsity Club, too. Remember," he teased her, "I got a letter in soccer and another one in tennis. I know I'm not all-state material like you are, but—"

Shelley cut him off. "So, have you thought about who you're going with? To the dance, I mean."

"Nah." He shook his head. "I don't know yet."

There was a long silence, and Shelley felt her stomach tighten into a knot. "I guess," she said slowly, "you haven't really thought about taking me."

"You?" Greg stared at her, surprised. The minute she saw the look on his face Shelley wanted desperately to take back what she had said. He looked stunned. He'd obviously never had even the slightest bit of romantic feeling for her.

"Never mind," Shelley mumbled quickly.

But Greg was so embarrassed that he made the situation worse by trying to joke about it. "We couldn't go together, Shel. I'm not tall enough for you. You need a guy like Patrick— someone who can tower over you on the dance floor." He laughed. "I mean, you're already taller than I am. And what if you wore high heels? We'd look ridiculous. I mean—"

Shelley felt her face turn bright red. "Forget it," she mumbled, her eyes filling with tears. "You're right."

She couldn't wait to get away from him. Here she had taken the biggest risk of her life and asked Greg Hilliard to the dance, and he'd made her feel like even more of a freak than she had felt before!

We'd look ridiculous. Those words kept repeating in her head as they walked the rest of the way home in awkward silence. He was right—they would, Shelley thought. But that was because she herself looked ridiculous. And she had asked him a ridiculous question.

She didn't even say hello to her mother when she got home. She ran straight upstairs and threw herself down on her bed and sobbed.

She was never going to forgive Greg. And she wasn't going back to those stupid dance lessons, either. As far as she was concerned, dancing was history. She wasn't going to go to the Varsity Club dance at all—not with Greg, not with anyone.

She wasn't going to be a laughingstock. If they wanted to give her an award, they would just have to send it to her.

Four

Gordon Tilman, the girls' basketball coach, blew his whistle and called the team over to him. It was Friday afternoon, and they had just finished their last workout before the first big playoff game.

"OK, you guys," Coach Tilman said, looking from one earnest face to the next. "I know you've heard me say this before, but we've got a tough team on our hands tomorrow. The only way we're going to beat Emerson is to play one hundred fifty percent. You with me?"

Everyone cheered. Cathy nudged Shelley, whose expression was vacant, and Shelley belatedly joined in the cheering.

Coach Tilman had apparently noticed. "Shelley, can I talk to you for a minute?" he asked after he told everyone to hit the showers and get a good night's sleep.

Hanging her head, Shelley nodded.

"Look," he said kindly, putting an arm around her shoulder, "I know you've got a lot of pressure on you. It isn't easy being an all-star player right before a big series begins. But somehow I'm getting the feeling that your heart hasn't been in the game these past few practices. Am I just imagining things, or is there something bugging you?"

Shelley blushed. "No, there's nothing wrong," she lied. "I guess I'm just a little nervous, that's all."

He gave her an affectionate pat on the back. "Well, remember, a lot of people are counting on you tomorrow. I heard through the grapevine that Ferini and some of the other college scouts are going to be at the game. If you play as well tomorrow as you have all season, I bet that scholarship to UCLA will be yours for the asking. Just play your best, and don't worry— it'll be great. Now get lost!"

When Shelley entered the locker room, Cathy was waiting for her at her locker. "What did Coach say?" she demanded.

"Nothing." Shelley wiped her face off with a towel. "I'm going to take a shower."

She brushed past her friend, knowing from

the look on Cathy's face that she had hurt her feelings. But she didn't feel like going into the whole thing right then. Why tell Cathy the terrible truth—that she'd broached the subject of the dance to Greg the other day; and he had made her feel awful?

Worse than awful, in fact. Shelley had never had a lot of confidence off the basketball court. But ever since Greg's harsh reaction, it seemed her confidence on the court was disappearing as well. She felt awkward and clumsy, as if her legs were too long and she was tripping over herself. And she felt heavier, too. It seemed to take forever to run from one end of the court to the other. The drills they did in practice felt unfamiliar to her, although she had been doing them for years. "I feel like an alien," Shelley muttered to herself in the shower. "A six-foot alien."

Cathy was waiting for Shelley when she came out of the locker room fifteen minutes later. "I've decided I'm walking home with you," Cathy announced, falling into step beside her.

Shelley didn't say anything.

"So, I take it you talked to Greg and it didn't go so well," Cathy said bluntly once they were walking down the sidewalk.

Shelley had to smile; Cathy knew her so well.

"Can we drop the subject? I've had enough humiliation for one week."

Cathy patted her on the arm. "I happen to be your best friend, remember? Things that hurt you hurt me." She narrowed her eyes in a menacing look. "Greg Hilliard's in big trouble if he hurt your feelings. Trust me."

Shelley couldn't help laughing. "Cut it out," she said affably. "Anyway, it isn't his fault that I'm a freak of nature."

Cathy was horrified. "He *said* that?"

Shelley shrugged. "Not in so many words. But, Cath . . ." Her voice trailed off. "You should've seen the look on his face when I asked him about the dance. That one look said it all. He looked like he was astonished that I'd even *think* of going with him."

"Greg Hilliard's a dope, then," Cathy said affectionately, linking her arm through Shelley's. "If he didn't die of joy on the spot, he's stupid. So forget him. Let's just go stag to the dance, OK?"

Shelley shook her head. "I don't think so." She knew Cathy was trying hard to make her feel better, but it wasn't working.

She couldn't erase the memory of Greg's expression when she had brought up the dance. Why couldn't she be cute and tiny and adorable like Carol? Or even *just* on the tall side, 5'9" like Cathy?

The past couple of days Shelley felt as if all the taunts she had heard in middle school were coming back to haunt her. Kids used to call her "towering inferno" because her hair was red. Or "the friendly giant." Or "Halfback Novak" because she was so good at sports. It was so embarrassing!

They reached the corner where Cathy had to turn right to go home and Shelley had to turn left. "Well," Cathy said, "I guess I'll see you tomorrow morning, huh?"

Shelley nodded. Cathy raised her right arm and made a fist—a secret victory sign the two girls had shared since they were little girls.

Sighing, Shelley lifted her own right arm and gave the signal back. But her heart wasn't in it. She knew she ought to be fired up about tomorrow morning's game, but instead, she was dreading it.

It was Saturday morning, and the first playoff game of the series between Sweet Valley High and Emerson was in the final quarter. It had been a tough game so far. Emerson had been leading at the half, 48–38, but in the third quarter Sweet Valley had come back, thanks to some incredible passing. Now, with only two minutes to go in the final quarter, the score was 78–76, Emerson leading.

Cathy had the ball and was racing down the court to Sweet Valley's basket, dribbling beautifully. "Shel!" Cathy cried, passing her the ball.

Shelley's heart was pounding. This was the sort of shot she had become famous for. She was far from the basket, but with her height and her precision. . . . She aimed carefully, trying to block out the sound of cheering coming from the bleachers. The ball sailed through the air and grazed the rim of the basket, bouncing backward right into the open arms of Nancy Roy, Emerson's best player. Shelley's eyes closed for an agonizing second as the Emerson fans all rose from the bleachers, screaming with joy. Nancy raced straight back to her own basket and dropped the ball in effortlessly. The score was 80–76, Emerson's lead widening with only fifty-eight seconds to go. Shelley felt sick. Her error would cost them the game.

Coach Tilman blew his whistle, calling a timeout. As Shelley jogged over to the huddle on the far side of the court, she noticed a boy in a green sweatshirt snapping photos of her. Instinctively she covered her face. She hated having her picture taken. And right now, after she had just missed a shot she should have made easily, the last thing she wanted was to have her picture taken. The guy lowered the camera, and she saw that it was the boy from dance class, Jim Roberts.

Coach Tilman gave them a short pep talk, not mentioning Shelley's missed shot. "You can do it, girls," he said. "We've still got time. Cathy, I want you to watch your blocking. Shel, be ready to catch passes and shoot for all you're worth." He passed around a water bottle and gave them all reassuring pats. "Don't let your energy slack off. We've got fifty-eight seconds, and we can still turn this game around!"

Shelley felt heartsick as she ran back out onto the court. She wished he had criticized her for messing up that shot instead of letting it go. She had disappointed the whole crowd. The thought of her parents and friends watching from up in the stands made her stomach churn. And Ferini and the other talent scouts. . . . She knew she looked terrible today. She just wanted the game to be over!

"Hey, relax," Cathy hissed. "This is a game, not a battle!"

But to Shelley it felt like a war, one she was going to lose.

The last fifty-eight seconds flew by. Emerson got control of the ball right away, and Sweet Valley couldn't get it away from them. Nancy scored two more baskets before the whistle blew: 84–76, Emerson.

Coach Tilman tried to console the team by focusing on the next game in the playoff series. "We'll get them back next Thursday," he said reassuringly. "I know it."

Shelley couldn't wait to get showered and changed and out of the locker room.

To her surprise and annoyance Jim Roberts was hanging around outside the locker room when she came out half an hour later. "Hi," he said shyly. "I just wanted to tell you—"

But Shelley was in no mood to be polite. "Look," she said, her voice sounding more rude than she had intended. "I just have one thing to say: I don't like having my picture taken. Do me a favor and dump that roll of film."

Jim looked embarrassed. "I didn't mean to upset you," he said.

Shelley nervously ruffled her short, wet hair with her fingers. "Well," she said, "you did." She didn't know what else to say.

"Why don't you like having your picture taken?" Jim went on.

Shelley stared at him. *What am I supposed to say to that? Because I have a bad self-image, Jim? Because I'm a klutz? Because I just missed the shot that could have turned the game around for us?*

"I was wondering," Jim blurted out, "if I

could take you out to get a soda or something. Or take a walk. You know."

Shelley was about to tell him she was tired and wanted to be alone when she saw Greg and Carol walk past, very much together, shoulders touching, staring into each other's eyes. "Jim, that sounds nice," she said loudly, so that Greg could hear her. "That's so sweet of you!"

Jim looked astonished. "You mean you'll come?"

Greg and Carol had passed by, and Shelley sighed heavily. She looked at Jim—really looked at him—and something in his earnest expression made her feel a little less rotten. He seemed like a sweet guy. And she didn't feel like going home to her parents, who would want to talk endlessly about the game and her strategy for the next one. Why not go out with Jim for a few hours? It wouldn't be the end of the world, and it might even be fun.

"Sure," she said, forcing a smile.

"I've got my car here," Jim said, fumbling to get his camera back into its case. "Let's go."

Shelley followed him out to the parking lot. "So," she said, "are you serious about photography? Most people don't lug expensive cameras around with them just for fun."

"No, I'm just a hack," Jim said, shrugging. "You know, I like snapping pictures. I like trying

47

to figure out how something's going to look on film and trying to capture things, places." He reddened a little. "I don't usually find people I want to take pictures of, though. But your face, the way you move—"

What was he trying to say? Shelley wondered.

"You're an amazingly graceful girl," he finished, avoiding her gaze. There was an awkward pause before he pointed out an old Camaro in the parking lot. "That's mine," he said with a self-effacing laugh.

Shelley didn't know what to say. She just followed him to the car, a million different thoughts colliding in her head.

Why hadn't she noticed him before? And was he serious, saying that stuff about her being graceful? Or was he just saying that so he could take more pictures of her?

Five

"These are fantastic," Elizabeth said, looking at a series of pictures Jeffrey had taken at the beach one rainy morning when it was deserted. They were in the darkroom, printing some of the photographs he had taken over the weekend. "I like the way the sand looks so grainy."

"Yeah, but I can't help thinking that these aren't really right," he said thoughtfully. "Do you know what I mean? I want to do something special for the competition, but I just haven't had a great idea yet."

Elizabeth nodded. Just then there was a knock on the door. "Come in, the coast is clear!" Jeffrey called out.

Jim Roberts tentatively stuck his head into the darkroom. "Hi. Mr. Collins told me I might be able to use the darkroom for a while to print some of my pictures." He looked shyly at Jeffrey and Elizabeth. "Can I print some stuff now, or are you two busy?"

"Help yourself," Jeffrey said, gesturing toward the pans filled with chemicals. "I'm finished." The darkroom was officially for the *Oracle* staff, but Mr. Collins occasionally let other students use it as long as they were considerate and neat.

Elizabeth looked curiously at Jim as he took negative files out of his backpack. "I didn't know you were a photographer, Jim."

Elizabeth wasn't really friends with Jim, but they had been introduced once or twice. She had always thought that he seemed like a really nice guy.

"Well, I just like to fool around a little. Nothing serious," Jim answered. "But Mr. Collins saw a photo I did, and he thought it was decent, so he said I could use the darkroom." He looked at the jars of solutions on the shelf. "It's such an expensive hobby. There's no way I could ever afford to develop and print all the rolls of stuff I shoot through a commercial lab."

"Yeah, I know what you mean," Jeffrey sympathized. Elizabeth watched Jim work with interest.

"Hey, this is great!" Jeffrey said, leaning over

and watching as one of Jim's photographs began to develop in the tray of solution. It was a portrait of an elderly woman bent over a little child, and Jim had done a wonderful job of capturing the woman's personality. Jeffrey shook his head in surprise. "You're a serious photographer. This is really good."

Jim looked embarrassed. "I just like to fool around," he repeated. "I've never taken real classes or anything. My dad gave me a camera when I was ten, and ever since then, I've been kind of addicted. I shoot several rolls of film a week." He laughed. "Sometimes I feel like I can't see things any other way than through a camera lens."

Elizabeth stared at the photograph of the old woman. She didn't want to be disloyal to Jeffrey, whose pictures were excellent, but Jim's work seemed to be of an entirely different caliber. "Let's see more," she urged him.

For the next hour they worked side by side, and all of Jim's photographs proved to be superb. He was an accomplished landscape photographer, but his best pictures were those of people. "Wow," Jeffrey said, looking at a photo of a little girl. "You can really capture someone on film. For me portraits are the hardest pictures to take. But yours just come to life!"

"I like taking pictures of people best," Jim admitted, lifting his last photo out of the developing solution and shaking it gently. Elizabeth stared at it. It was a shot of a young woman leaping up to sink a basketball into a hoop.

"This is beautiful," she breathed. "Jim, who is this? She looks familiar."

Jim blushed. "Oh. That's Shelley Novak," he said. He studied the photograph with interest.

Elizabeth couldn't get over what an amazing shot it was. "This is fantastic," she enthused. "She looks so graceful—like she's floating on air or something."

"You should take more pictures of her. She's a really good subject for you," Jeffrey said.

Jim shook his head. "Nah," he said, lifting the photograph up to dry. "I don't think so."

Jeffrey looked thoughtfully at the picture of Shelley. "Did Mr. Collins tell you about the photography contest the *News* is sponsoring?"

"Yeah, he said something about it." Jim didn't seem thrilled by the idea. "But I'm not really up for something like that. Photography is just something I like to do for myself."

"You should enter it," Jeffrey said. Elizabeth smiled, thinking how characteristic it was for Jeffrey to encourage Jim to enter, even though it would diminish his own chances of winning.

"Jeffrey's right," she agreed. "You're really talented, Jim. You should definitely submit something to the *News*. I think you have a good chance of winning."

But Jim shook his head. "I don't think so. I just do it for fun—for me. I don't really feel like entering any contest."

Elizabeth caught Jeffrey's eye. She wondered if he was thinking what she was.

Jim appeared to be an extremely talented photographer. Why wasn't he more interested in this opportunity to show other people how good he was?

"I've never been up here before," Shelley said, staring down at the breathtaking view of Sweet Valley from Miller's Point. When Jim had suggested taking a ride after practice on Tuesday, she'd been reluctant at first. But because she had had such a good time with him after the game on Saturday, she changed her mind. Now she was really glad she had.

"It's like seeing a whole new world," she said, her eyes shining.

Jim snapped several shots with his Nikon. "I love it up here. One of the coolest things about a camera is the way you can catch things from different angles. That's why I love going to out-of-the-way places." He grinned at her. "My parents always tease me. Whenever we go on trips, I want to climb to the highest place I can find so I can get a panoramic picture." He laughed. "That bugs them. But even worse, I want to time our visits to places so the light's hitting things in a certain way."

Shelley started to laugh, too. "That would be kind of annoying."

Jim ducked behind a bush, dropped to one knee, and aimed his camera at her. "Smile!" he cried.

The smile on Shelley's face disappeared. "Come on, cut it out," she said, trying to keep her voice light.

Jim snapped three pictures in a row. "You're beautiful when you're mad," he teased her.

But Shelley felt angry, even though she knew he was only being nice. "I mean it, Jim. I don't want my picture taken!"

"Why?" He lowered the camera and stared at her.

Shelley shrugged. "Let's just say I have a kind of phobia about it. OK?"

Jim came closer to her, a concerned look on his face. "Wow, you're really serious about this, aren't you?"

Shelley nodded. "I can't stand having my

picture taken. Please promise me you won't show those pictures to anyone."

"Sure," Jim said casually, putting the lens cap back on his camera.

"No—promise. Really promise," she pleaded.

Jim looked her in the eyes. His expression was so intense that Shelley was afraid he was mad at her. "All right," he said after a long pause. "I promise, Shelley." He put his camera down. "If I knew it bugged you so much, I wouldn't have done it. I was just fooling around."

Shelley didn't answer. She didn't want Jim to hear how upset she was. Why couldn't she just relax and let him take her picture? she scolded herself. *Because I don't photograph well. Because I'm all legs.*

Jim suddenly reached out and touched her face, running his finger along her cheek. She could barely breathe, his touch was so gentle. "But you're so beautiful," he whispered. "Why don't you want to let me capture that beauty on film?"

Shelley stared at him. No one had ever touched her like that before. Part of her wanted to freeze, to stay absolutely still so he wouldn't stop. But almost despite herself she jerked back. "I can't help it. I'm just shy," she said lamely.

Jim didn't say anything, and after a minute or

two they walked back to his Camaro, each knowing it was time to head home. Shelley kept quiet all the way there.

She couldn't stop thinking about Jim's touch. Every minute or two she sneaked a glance at him out of the corner of her eye. He wasn't one bit like Greg, and to be honest, she never would have thought of him romantically. He was a funny guy, alternately lighthearted and intense. But she really liked Jim. They had fun together, and it felt easy and natural to spend time with him.

"I want to see you again," he said when they reached her house. "Will you let me take you out later this week? Maybe we could go to a movie or something on Friday night."

Shelley nodded, still afraid to speak and reveal her feelings.

She was sure she liked Jim, a lot, and she thought he liked her, too. The question was, how did they like each other? Were they just friends, or was something else going on between them?

"I just can't tell," Shelley told Cathy the next day at lunch. "I think he's amazingly nice, and I feel like I can tell him anything. He's so easy to talk to. But I just don't think he's . . . you know . . ."

"What?" Cathy asked with a smile. "He's not Greg Hilliard."

"No, that isn't what I meant," Shelley said quickly. In fact, what Cathy had said wasn't far from the truth.

But Shelley really didn't want to talk about her pathetic love life at the moment. "Look, there's no use comparing the two of them, because I'm sure Jim isn't interested in me that way, anyway," she said hastily. "He just wants to be friends."

"Well, I have to go look up some stuff in the library," Cathy said, crumpling her lunch bag into a ball. "Want to come, or are you going to stay here?"

Shelley had just caught sight of Jim on the other side of the cafeteria, his camera with him, as always. "I'm going to go say hi to Jim," she said lightly.

"Uh-huh," Cathy said knowingly.

Shelley ignored her, stood up, and crossed the crowded dining hall toward Jim. "Hey," she said, pulling up a chair.

Jim's face lit up when he saw her. "Shelley, hi! I was just thinking about you."

Shelley's stomach did a flip-flop. It was nice to have someone look so happy to see her.

"I printed those pictures I took of you yesterday. Shel, you should see them. You look absolutely amazing. I swear you could be a model. You look so graceful."

Shelley frowned. Why did he have to ruin everything by reminding her about those pictures he'd taken? "I told you," she said abruptly, "I can't stand being photographed." She tried not to look at his camera lying on the table between them.

"Won't you even look at these?" Jim asked. "Honestly, Shelley, if you see how beautiful you look in them, I know you'll change your mind."

"I'd love to look at your pictures—as long they're not of me," she said firmly. Then she looked anxiously at him. "You haven't shown them to anyone else, have you? Remember, you promised not to."

"I remember," Jim said quietly. He covered her hand with his on the table. "Don't worry, Shel. I promise I won't mention them again. And I won't take any more pictures of you, either."

Shelley could tell he meant it. And for that minute, with his hand on hers, she had a glimpse of what it felt like to trust somebody. She could barely bring herself to lift her eyes and look at him.

She knew Jim Roberts would never hurt her. It was a brand-new feeling for Shelley, and one she wanted to savor. She was just afraid that if she looked at him, he'd be able to tell what she was feeling.

Shelley wasn't ready for that yet. Not quite. But it was still something to realize that she trusted him. And that she liked him, definitely liked him, and not just as a friend, either!

Six

"I can't wait till this afternoon," Jessica whispered to Amy in chemistry lab. "I know I'm going to get Patrick to dance with me. I just know it."

Amy's brow wrinkled as she attempted to concentrate on the experiment they were doing. "I can't stand science," she muttered. She gave Jessica a despairing look. "Can't you stop talking about Patrick and help me do whatever we're supposed to be doing?"

Jessica ignored her. "You're just jealous because you realize that Patrick really has the hots for me and not you."

"Right," Amy snapped. "He's so crazy about you, and that's why he asked Too-Tall Novak to be his dance partner last week."

"That was nothing," Jessica retorted. "She

was just nearer the front of the room, that's all. *You* blew it when you asked him for pointers on the box step, and you know it. Don't you care that you made a fool of yourself in front of everyone?"

Amy raised her eyebrows. "For your information, *I* wasn't the one who made a fool of myself. *You* were the one who had to horn in on us and—"

"Girls," Mr. Russo, their science teacher, said reprovingly. He came over to the table. "You know, neither of you can afford to fall behind on this project. Am I going to have to ask you two to start coming in on your lunch hours to work, or can I count on you to be serious during lab?"

"You can count on us to be serious, Mr. Russo," Amy said, using the sickeningly sweet voice she reserved for teachers.

Jessica waited until Mr. Russo had returned to his desk before speaking. "Just wait till the next dance class," she whispered. "You'll see."

"No, you'll see—me in Patrick's arms," Amy hissed.

But Jessica just smiled blithely as she opened her lab book and made a notation. "Jealous, jealous, jealous," she murmured.

* * *

Already news had spread through the school that the ballroom dance lessons in the gym were being taught by one of the sexiest men anyone had ever seen. Jessica had hoped people would keep quiet about it, since the last thing she wanted was for a whole crowd of girls to come between her and Patrick. But by four o'clock more than fifty girls had made their way into the gym to get a look at him.

Even Lila Fowler, the richest girl in the whole school, had decided it might be worth brushing up on her waltzing skills—if Patrick McLean was *that* handsome.

"Wow!" Patrick exclaimed, looking at the crowd with a big smile. "What happened? How come ballroom dancing got so popular around here all of a sudden?"

Lila, standing between Amy and Jessica, seemed impressed. "You guys are right," she conceded. "He's absolutely gorgeous!"

She spoke louder than she had intended, and everyone heard her, including Patrick.

"Way to go, Lila," Jessica said with a giggle.

Amy looked mortified. "You two are so immature," she said, stepping away so it didn't look as if she were with them.

Patrick was smiling at Lila and Jessica, probably trying to figure out who had spoken. Jessica felt her face turn red. Did he think *she* had said it? She was getting ready to run from the room to spare herself further humiliation when Patrick said, "You, in the blue shirt. How would you like to let me try the tango out on you?"

Jessica could hardly believe her luck. "See?" she said to Amy as she flounced past her to the front of the room. "I told you so!"

From now on, she thought, blue was going to be her lucky color. And the tango was going to be *their* dance—hers and Patrick's. When they'd been married for years, they could tell their children about it.

"Now listen up, everybody," Patrick said. "This isn't an easy dance. Do you all remember the box step I showed you last time?"

The handful of people who'd been at last Wednesday's lesson cried, "Yes!" But Jessica couldn't remember anything about it. Not when she was standing this close to Patrick, who was wearing an after-shave lotion that she found incredibly sexy.

"Now, watch where I put my hand on—" He looked down at Jessica. "What's your name?"

Jessica practically melted. "Jessica," she breathed.

"OK. Watch where I put my hand on Jessica's back." He pivoted Jessica, his hand on the small of her back. Jessica was in complete heaven. She tried to catch Amy's eye so she could show her how deliriously happy she was.

But as soon as the tango music started, Jessica's happiness disappeared. Patrick was moving her this way and that so fast, she had no idea what was happening. Instead of gliding across the floor in his arms, she was stepping all over his feet. "Sorry," she muttered every time it happened.

"Just relax," Patrick gasped, pushing her backward and pulling her forward. "Just—go—with—the—*music!*"

Jessica's hands were sweaty, and her face was hot. This was awful. If this was what she was going to have to go through to dance with Patrick, maybe she wasn't quite ready for him yet.

But there was no point showing anyone else how she felt. When Amy and Lila pumped her for information later, Jessica made it sound like the best five minutes of her entire life. "He's so wonderful to hold," she said languidly. "I could've danced forever."

"Yeah?" Amy said skeptically. "How come it looked like you two were kicking each other the whole time?"

Jessica rolled her eyes at her friend. "Amy, you don't understand anything. That happens to be the way the tango is done," she snapped.

She couldn't wait to get out of there. All of a

sudden she had a sinking feeling that ballroom dancing might not be her thing after all.

At Thursday's game Shelley was sure she had never played basketball so well in her entire life. She felt as if she were running on air, and she obviously wasn't the only one feeling so light-footed. Somehow the team had gotten their old magic back, and by halftime they were leading Emerson 62–38. Coach Tilman couldn't believe it. "You guys are amazing!" he cried, throwing his arm around Shelley's shoulders. "And you—I can't get over the way you're playing. You're turning into some kind of shooting machine out there." His eyes were glowing, but Shelley thought he looked a little concerned, too. "Just promise me you won't burn out. We need you to hang on to some reserve strength. This looks like it may be a long series."

Shelley barely heard him. She was in her own private world. There were only two things she was aware of: the basketball game and Jim Roberts. Jim, whom she could see on the sidelines, was cheering her on with every step. Every cheer from him seemed to give her a strength and grace she had never known before.

"Whatever you're doing, just keep it up," Cathy told her.

Shelley grinned. "I think maybe I will," she said. The whistle blew then, and they ran out to finish the game—an easy victory at 86–64.

Jim was waiting for her afterward. "Promise you'll let me take you out to celebrate," he begged.

Shelley's eyes were shining. "Oh, all right. I'll let you." She grinned. She couldn't believe how good it was to see him and how great it felt when he slipped his arm around her.

That evening ended up being one of the most wonderful Shelley had ever spent. Jim took her out for a victory pizza, and then they drove down to the beach to look at the moon. "I can't get over how gorgeous you looked out there," Jim said, taking her hand in his.

Shelley took a deep breath. Here they were, just the two of them, with the moonlight shimmering on the ocean. Nobody else was in sight. It felt funny to be walking so close to Jim, their shoulders brushing. They both slipped out of their shoes so they could walk in the water, and Shelley had the urge to pinch herself to prove this was really happening.

"You know, you're not like any girl I've ever met before," Jim said seriously. "It's like—well, this is kind of hard to explain. But you're so easy to be with. You don't play games like a lot of girls do. You don't seem obsessed with makeup or flirting or any of that stuff. You just seem totally natural." His voice was husky. "At first I just wanted to get to know you because I loved watching you play basketball. And because you seemed different to me. More *yourself* than so many girls are." His voice caught. "But, Shel—"

She stopped walking, and he pulled her to him, both his arms around her now. He was staring straight into her eyes, and Shelley couldn't help thinking, *We're* exactly *the same height.*

Jim seemed to be reading her mind. "We kind of see eye to eye, huh," he teased, leaning forward so their noses bumped.

Shelley tilted her face up inquisitively, and the next thing she knew his mouth was brushing hers, his kiss soft and tender. They broke apart and stared at each other. Then at the same minute they let go of the shoes they had been carrying and hugged each other hard, then kissed each other with an intensity that neither had ever known.

"Jim, listen to me," Jeffrey said on Friday morning at school. He picked up one of the photographs that Jim had hung up in the darkroom to dry. "I don't want to keep going on and on about this, but I really think you should enter a photograph in the *News* contest." He looked more closely at the photo in his hand. "This one," he added, handing it to Jim.

Jim frowned. "No," he said, putting the photograph down. It was one he'd taken of Shelley the day before at the second playoff game. She was jumping up for a basket, her face partly obscured, her arms and legs long and graceful. It was an amazingly good shot, and he knew it captured what was most striking about Shelley: the ease with which she played the game, combined with her very special athletic beauty. It was probably the best picture he had ever taken.

He shouldn't have taken it, though. He had promised Shelley he wouldn't. But he had his camera with him, and when he saw her playing such a great game, he couldn't resist snapping a few shots.

"Look," Jeffrey said matter-of-factly, "if you enter this photograph, you could win. Do you realize how great it would be to get this published? The deadline to enter is noon today. If you win, you get your picture published next Friday." He shook his head. "You could make some money from your photography, Jim. You're really talented. It's a shame to hide it."

Jim tried to change the subject. "Hey, how come you're so big on getting me to enter this thing? Don't you want to win it yourself? Your work is pretty good, too."

But Jeffrey wasn't about to be distracted. "Look, if you were an athlete like Shelley, do you think you would just sit on the sidelines? No way. You would be out there playing. It's the same for you with photography."

"It isn't—" Jim started to protest.

Jeffrey shrugged his shoulders and said, "It's up to you. I'm not going to force you." And with that he picked up his photographs and put them in his backpack. "Just remember, twelve noon today is the cutoff time. And I happen to think you ought to go for it."

Jim watched the door swing closed behind Jeffrey. He picked up the photograph of Shelley, and a smile crossed his face. It gave him so much pleasure to look at it. What a beautiful girl she was!

All of a sudden the desire to see Shelley's picture on the front page of the *News* next week was so strong, he almost couldn't resist it. Wouldn't it make Shelley realize once and for all that she really was beautiful? That she had a way of moving that the rest of the world admired?

Seven

At lunchtime on Friday, Elizabeth and Olivia Davidson, the arts editor of *The Oracle*, were doing some last-minute work on the following week's edition of the newspaper.

"Did Jeffrey submit something to the *News* competition?" Olivia asked, looking over at the box Mr. Collins had set up at one end of the office. Submissions had to be in by noon, just five minutes away.

Elizabeth nodded. "He was pretty torn. He had a landscape shot, a really beautiful picture he took in Oregon before he moved here, and a more recent photograph of some kids downtown. He finally decided to go with the more recent one, which I think was a good idea."

"Well, I bet he's got a pretty good chance at winning," Olivia said loyally.

Just then the door to the office opened, and Jim Roberts stuck his head inside. "Oh—hi," he said shyly. "I didn't think anyone would be in here. I just wanted to drop off a submission for that photography contest."

Elizabeth was surprised and pleased. She didn't think Jim was going to enter anything. He must have changed his mind at the last minute, she thought.

Olivia was crossing the room to the copy machine. She stopped when she saw Jim frowning critically at the photograph he had slipped out of a manila envelope. She walked up behind him. "Wow, that's a terrific photograph," she said, staring at the picture.

Jim's face turned red, and he stuffed the photograph back into the envelope. "Thanks," he mumbled. Without another word he dropped the envelope into the submissions box.

"He's talented," Olivia said to Elizabeth after Jim had left.

"I know." Elizabeth was about to fill Olivia in on some of the conversations she and Jeffrey had had with Jim over the past week or two when the telephone rang. It was Roger Collins, asking Elizabeth if she could bring the box of photographs to his office for him. Someone from the *News* was there to collect them.

"I'll meet you in the lunchroom," Elizabeth told Olivia. "Mr. Collins wants me to bring these to him right away."

Olivia nodded. A few minutes later she had slung her backpack over her shoulder and headed down the hall to the lunchroom, deep in thought. She was wondering why Jim had never submitted work to the school paper. As arts editor, she was always excited when she found out one of her classmates was really talented. Why hadn't she known anything about Jim Roberts's skill as a photographer before now?

Olivia picked up a tray in line, still deep in thought. To her surprise she saw Shelley Novak in line in front of her. She didn't know Shelley very well, but she had been following Shelley's success during the basketball season, and she had developed a tremendous amount of respect for her.

"Hi," she said, stepping into line behind the tall girl. She smiled as she looked at Shelley's nutritious choice of lunch foods: yogurt, a fruit salad, and iced tea. "No wonder you're so fit, eating like that! Don't you have to eat more just to keep your weight even?"

Shelley laughed. "I gain weight easily, so I have to be careful during the season not to gain anything. All I need is to have to run with extra pounds on me."

Olivia shook her head admiringly. "Well, you're obviously doing something right. You probably have no idea how graceful you look on the court. If you could see the photograph I just saw, you'd know what I mean."

Shelley frowned at Olivia. "Oh? What photograph is that?" she asked.

"Oh, something someone submitted to the *News* competition. It's this gorgeous shot of you leaping up to make a basket." Olivia helped herself to a salad. "I'll bet you anything it wins."

Olivia reached into her shoulder bag for her wallet to pay for lunch. When she looked back up at Shelley, Olivia couldn't help thinking she had offended her somehow.

Shelley looked absolutely furious. Her eyes were flashing with anger.

"I didn't say anything wrong, did I?" Olivia asked uneasily.

Shelley shook her head. "No, Olivia. You didn't say anything wrong. Don't worry, it isn't you I'm mad at." And with that she swept off with her tray, her head held high.

"Shelley?" Jim called. It was three-thirty, and the last bell of the day had just rung. Jim had been trying to find Shelley between classes all afternoon. He knew she had practice at four, and he wanted to make sure he knew what time to pick her up that evening. They had plans to go out to dinner.

Shelley didn't turn around, and Jim hurried to catch up with her.

"Shel!" he called.

Shelley heard him but tried her hardest to act as if she hadn't. *What a jerk*, she thought. *First he humiliates me by submitting that picture to the contest, then he chases me down the hall, calling out my name. Does he want everything between us to be public, or does he just love embarrassing me like everyone else?*

"Wait up," Jim gasped as he got closer. "Remember, we're not all star athletes. Give a guy a break!"

They had reached the end of the hallway, where Shelley had to turn to go down to the locker room. She stopped, then took a deep breath to steady herself. "Listen, Jim. I really don't think you and I have anything to say to each other," she said as coldly as she could.

Jim stared at her. "What?" he cried. "Shelley, what do you— "

But Shelley didn't let him finish. "I trusted you," she snapped. "When you made that promise to me, I believed you." Her eyes filled with tears. "I guess I was an idiot, right? I should've known better. I should've guessed you were only spending time with me because—" Her voice broke. "Because you wanted to take my picture for that ridiculous contest."

Jim looked anguished. "I knew I never should've turned that thing in." he said. "Shel, I'm so sorry. I was the idiot, I admit it. But if you'd just let me explain—"

"There's nothing to explain," Shelley said, her voice tight with anger. She felt a wave of disappointment wash over her. Up until that minute she had still been hoping that it was all a mistake, that Olivia was wrong, that Jim really hadn't been the one to turn in the photograph. But he'd said it himself—he'd done it. "We had a promise, Jim. You broke it. What else is there for us to say to each other?"

Jim looked as if he was in agony. "Come on, Shelley. Give me a chance to explain to you what happened. Did it ever occur to you that it wasn't my idea to submit that picture to the contest?"

"I don't care whose idea it was." Shelley crossed her arms, her eyes flashing. "You're old enough to make up your own mind. You promised me that you'd never take a picture of me again—and that you'd never show it to anyone if you did." She glared at him. "So what do you do? You enter a picture of me in a contest, hoping it'll get published—so the whole world can laugh at me instead of just you and Olivia Davidson!"

Now Jim was starting to get angry, too. "Shelley, you're being ridiculous. No one is laughing at you. The whole reason—"

Once again Shelley cut him off. "Don't you dare call me ridiculous! You're the one who's trying to make me look like a fool by taking a picture of me and plastering it all over the papers!"

Jim shook his head wearily. "Look, we're both being unreasonable," he tried.

"You broke your promise," she cried, her eyes shining with tears. "I don't care what else you say, Jim. How can I ever trust you again?" And with that she spun on her heel and ran down the hallway toward the locker room.

She couldn't believe she had really thought Jim was different. Well, she had learned her lesson now. She'd been out of her mind to think Jim really cared about her. Maybe it was just as well she found out now—before it really hurt.

But the hot tears spilling down her cheeks told her that it was too late: it hurt already.

*   *   *

"All right," Cathy said with a sigh after practice. "Are you going to tell me what's wrong, or do I have to figure it out by myself? Because I will, you know, sooner or later."

Shelley was putting an ice pack on her left ankle, which had been swelling up after practice. "I don't want to talk about it," she mumbled.

"All right, then, I'll have to use my mental telepathy," Cathy said, squeezing her eyes shut. When she opened them, she gave her friend a sympathetic smile. "Something tells me it's you and Jim. Am I warm?"

"You're warm. You're more than warm," Shelley said with a groan. "All right, I'll tell you the whole depressing story. But you have to promise not to lecture me for having convinced myself this guy was worth caring about."

She filled Cathy in on the photography contest, Jim's promise, and the news Olivia had broken to her that day at lunch. Cathy listened avidly.

"So," Cathy said when Shelley was through, "you're mad because Jim didn't ask your permission first to enter the picture. Right?"

"I'm not mad," Shelley said. "I'm furious! We had a promise, Cath, and he deliberately broke it."

Cathy nodded. "I can see why you'd be upset. But it seems to me that maybe you could tell him how you feel and talk it through with him. He seems like such a nice guy.''

Shelley stared at her. ''I can't believe this. My own best friend takes *his* side,'' she complained. ''Don't you realize what an incredible breach of trust this is? I mean, I ask Jim not to take pictures of me, not to show anyone, and he—''

''OK, OK,'' Cathy said quickly. ''I understand. It's just that I wonder whether you've really given Jim a chance to explain, that's all. Maybe he's got a reason for all this that he hasn't told you about yet.''

Shelley didn't answer for a minute. ''I think I gave him a chance. There's no denying the fact that he broke his promise.''

''Fair enough.'' Cathy shrugged. ''But maybe— well, maybe this competition was really important to him. Try to imagine how you'd feel if he asked you not to play basketball. Wouldn't you be upset?''

''Cathy, that's absurd. It isn't the same thing at all. I never asked him not to take pictures, just not to take pictures of *me*.''

Cathy nodded. ''That's true. Still,'' she added, ''it sounds to me like you may be overreacting a little. Shelley, why does it bug you so much to let him take your picture?''

Shelley's eyes stung with tears. She couldn't look her friend in the face. "You know why," she said at last. She practically had to choke out the words.

"No, I don't. I want to understand, though," Cathy urged her friend. "Try to explain it to me."

A single tear rolled down Shelley's cheek. "Because I'm a freak, that's why! Because I look like a giraffe. Remember the nickname 'towering inferno'? That's how people see me. I can't stand the thought of everyone laughing at me!"

Cathy shook her head in disbelief. "And you really think Jim wanted to take your picture because he thinks you look like a freak? Shelley, you're out of your mind. You happen to be a beautiful girl. You're tall, but so what? So are half the top fashion models in the world. You're willowy and graceful, and you're incredibly photogenic." Her voice was firm. "My guess is that Jim found you were an exceptional subject, and he was probably torn up about what to do with his picture."

Shelley pretended to concentrate on the ice pack she was holding against her ankle. "I can see why he'd want to compete in the contest. That makes sense to me. Maybe I didn't understand before how serious photography is to him,

79

because he's sort of minimized it to me. But I can't understand his breaking his promise to me, Cathy. I just can't.''

Her friend shrugged. ''Well, only you know how you feel about him. You two haven't been going out for very long. If you don't think he's worth talking this out with, that's your business.'' Cathy paused and looked at Shelley seriously. ''But I think you have a problem with your self-image, Shelley. And that isn't going to go away just by not speaking to Jim. It's something you're going to have to deal with by yourself.''

Shelley didn't answer. She couldn't. She was afraid her voice would betray how upset she was if she said even one word.

Shelley knew Cathy was right. She had overreacted to Jim's pictures because she was certain there was something wrong with her. Deep down she knew it was irrational, but she couldn't help it.

Maybe that was why she had been so quick to feel betrayed by Jim, because it was so hard for her to believe any guy could really find her attractive.

Maybe she *had* been too hasty about Jim. She had spent her whole life in competition, and she knew how important it was to win something that really mattered.

She wasn't happy that Jim had used a picture of her against her wishes. But maybe she shouldn't have blown up at him the way she did.

She bent over her ankle, hiding her face from Cathy. It might not be too late, she told herself. She could still call Jim and tell him that she was sorry.

Eight

"Shelley!" Mrs. Novak yelled up the stairs. "The phone's for you!"

Shelley jumped to her feet. It was eight o'clock Friday evening, and she had been tense ever since she got home from practice, trying to decide whether or not to call Jim. Naturally she assumed their plans to go out to dinner were off. And Jim, she thought, must have assumed the same thing, because by eight o'clock she still hadn't heard from him, and they had agreed to go out at seven-thirty.

"Hello?" Shelley said nervously into the phone.

"Hey, Shel. Have you called him yet?" Cathy asked.

Shelley's heart sank. "Oh—it's you," she said, not bothering to hide her disappointment.

"I guess that means you haven't," Cathy went on. "Shelley, break down and call the poor guy! One of you is going to have to be the one to make up."

Shelley anxiously twisted the phone cord around one finger. Part of her agreed with her friend. But every time she thought about Jim entering that photograph in the contest, she got angry all over again.

"All right, I'll call him," she said.

As soon as Shelley hung up, she dialed Jim's number. She had called Information earlier that evening to get the number, since she'd never called him before, but then she chickened out. This time she had to go through with it. "Is Jim there?" she asked when a girl answered the phone.

"Yeah, just a minute," the girl said. Shelley guessed it must be his sister.

"Hello?" Jim said a minute later. His voice sounded funny, and Shelley realized then that they had never even spoken to each other on the phone before.

"Jim, it's me, Shelley," she said. Then she paused to take a deep breath. There were a lot of things she wanted to say. She wanted to apologize for blowing up and making a scene and not giving him the chance to explain himself. She wanted to let him know how much she liked him and how sorry she was that they had gotten into a big fight. But somehow nothing came out of her mouth. She was completely silent, struggling to find the right words.

Jim cleared his throat. "I was just about to call you," he said. His voice sounded dull and unnatural. "I want to apologize again for going back on my word. You were right, Shelley, and I was wrong."

Shelley started to protest. "But—"

"Wait," he said. "Just let me finish. The reason I was going to call was to tell you that you don't have to panic about that picture. I stopped by Mr. Collins's office after school and told him I wanted it withdrawn from the competition. He was a little angry about it, but I told him it was an emergency, that there was no way that picture could be in the contest. So he called up his friend at the *News*, and they said they'd take it out."

Shelley couldn't believe it. "You took it out of the running? But, Jim—"

"So you don't have to worry," Jim repeated flatly. "Anyway, I'm sorry I got you so upset. I really didn't mean to."

Shelley's stomach was churning. She felt terrible. Jim's voice sounded like a stranger's, cold and harsh. "You didn't have to do that," she said, aware of how pointless she sounded. After all, he had only done it because *she* had made such a fuss.

"Well, it's all over now, so we can both just forget it," Jim said. "I guess I'll see you next week in school." Before Shelley could say another word, Jim hung up the phone.

Shelley slowly put the receiver down. She had to blink hard to keep the tears from coming. "Well," she said out loud, "he's right. It's all over now." She got to her feet and walked across the room to her mirror. Looking at her reflection, she shook her head. Whatever Jim had seen as beautiful or graceful in her just wasn't there.

Had she been crazy to try so hard to convince him that she wasn't beautiful, that she wasn't worth photographing?

She couldn't think about Jim without a feeling of anguish. Something really important had started between them. *Leave it to me*, Shelley thought, *to take something wonderful and turn it into a royal mess.*

"Well," Cathy said philosophically, finishing the pineapple-orange juice she had ordered at the outdoor café where she and Shelley were sitting on Saturday afternoon, "it sounds to me like you really can't do much right now. You're just going to have to wait to see Jim in school next week."

"He didn't even come to the game this morning," Shelley despaired. Sweet Valley had beaten Emerson in the third playoff game, making the series score two games to one, with Sweet Valley leading. Next Friday could be the deciding game if Sweet Valley won for the third time in a row. "I never thought I'd be saying this, but I actually looked for him on the sidelines—and for his camera—and I was crushed when he wasn't there. I would have even put up with having my picture taken!"

Cathy patted her hand. "At least one good thing's come out of this. You know how strongly you feel about him," she told Shelley.

Shelley nodded sadly. She reached into her pocket for change and laid it on top of the bill the waitress had brought them. "I have to get going," she said. "I have an errand to run."

Ten minutes later Shelley was leaning her bike against the garage adjoining Mr. Collins's attractive ranch house where he lived with his son, Teddy. Shelley had done some baby-sitting for Teddy, so she didn't feel uncomfortable going over to the Collinses' house to talk. And she thought Mr. Collins would understand once she explained why she was there. She rang the door bell, then shifted her weight nervously from one foot to the other as she waited.

"Shelley! What brings you here on a beautiful afternoon like this?" Mr. Collins asked, giving her a warm smile and opening the door wider to let her in. "I thought you'd be out with the rest of the team, celebrating that wonderful victory you earned this morning."

Shelley bit her lip. "Well, I'm going to go out with the team tonight. But I wanted to ask you something, and I thought it would be better if I came over and talked to you about it in person."

Mr. Collins nodded. "Well, Teddy's out riding his bike with some friends. Can I get you a cold drink? Iced tea or something?"

"No, thanks." Shelley sat down in the chair he offered her and tried not to wring her hands. "Listen, I know this is going to sound kind of odd, but I was wondering whether or not it's too late to put Jim Roberts's picture back in the *News* competition."

Mr. Collins looked surprised. "Well," he said slowly, after a moment's thought, "I think Jim felt quite strongly about taking it out. I wouldn't want to complicate things even further by reentering it without his permission." He looked gravely at Shelley. "Did you and Jim talk about this?"

Shelley looked down at the floor. "You know the picture is of me, right?"

"No," Mr. Collins said. "The only thing I know about it is that Jim asked me to withdraw it."

Shelley sighed. "Well, it's all my fault. Jim took some shots of me playing basketball, and I asked him not to show them to anyone. I've always been kind of"—she faltered—"self-conscious about my height. I know it sounds dumb, but I just don't like having my picture taken."

"I can understand that," Mr. Collins said gently. He smiled at her. "I think we're all afraid of the things that make us stand out from other people." He cleared his throat. "The funny thing is, it's usually the things we're most embarrassed about that are the very things other people envy in us."

"Well," Shelley said, twisting a ring on her little finger, "I made Jim promise not to show anyone those pictures. And he ended up entering one of them in the contest without telling me about it. So I blew up at him." She stared at Mr. Collins, waiting for him to be shocked. But he didn't seem to be.

"And that's when Jim asked me to take the picture out of the contest," he mused. "Well, that explains a lot." He stared at her. "Except for one thing: Why do you want the picture to go back in?"

Shelley frowned. "It's hard to explain. When I was playing this morning, I kept thinking about competition. When you play a lot of sports, you take competition pretty seriously. You know what it means to put all of yourself into something you want. I think Jim deserves recognition for his photography, and I think he ought to compete." She shrugged. "I'm sorry there was a misunderstanding between him and me, but I don't think that ought to ruin his chances in the contest."

Mr. Collins smiled broadly at her. "You're a real grown-up, Shelley," he said quietly. "What you just said shows true selflessness. I think Jim Roberts is lucky to have you for a friend."

Yeah, Shelley thought. *Only we're not friends anymore.*

"So, can you put the picture back in the contest?" she asked.

Mr. Collins got to his feet. "I'll call my friend at the *News* right away and see what we can do." He winked at her. "Something tells me we might be able to get it back in the running."

For the rest of the weekend, Shelley tried not to think about Jim. But the harder she tried to get him out of her mind, the more she kept replaying that scene with him in the hallway on Friday. Maybe on Monday, she thought, once they were back in school, she could explain herself and apologize.

But the first thing Monday morning, when she ran into Jim in the hallway, it became clear that the cold war between them was still going strong. Jim said hi and just walked past, not even stopping to talk. Shelley was so mad at Jim for ignoring her that when she ran into him in the lunchroom, she walked right past him, giving just a little nod of her head to show that she had seen him.

"What's going on with you two? I've seen you be friendlier to the forward on Emerson's team than you're being to poor Jim Roberts," Cathy whispered as the two girls walked to practice together that afternoon. Jim and Shelley had just passed each other in the hallway again—this time barely acknowledging each other.

Shelley frowned. "He doesn't want to talk to me," she said flatly. "What else can I do?"

"How do you know he doesn't? Maybe he thinks you don't want to talk to him," Cathy reasoned.

Shelley shook her head. "Forget it, Cath. I know what I know. He and I are totally finished —through—kaput. So let's not talk about him anymore, OK?"

Cathy wrinkled her nose. "OK," she conceded. "I guess that means you and I are still going to the Varsity Club dance together this Friday, huh?"

Shelley groaned. The dance was the last thing she wanted to think about at the moment.

"Cathy," she said, "let's just try to get through one thing at a time, all right?"

What she didn't tell her friend was that she felt as if her heart was breaking. The truth was, she missed Jim. She wanted more than anything in the world to chase after him and tell him how she really felt.

But her pride was far too great for that. And from the look of things, so was his.

Nine

Elizabeth and Jeffrey were sitting together in study hall when Mr. Collins came into the lounge with a big smile on his face. "Jeffrey," he said, "I have some news for you. Can you come down to my office for a few minutes?"

Elizabeth's pulse raced. The *News* contest! Could they have heard already? It was only Wednesday, and the winning photograph wouldn't be published until Friday, but maybe the winner had already been announced. She gave Jeffrey's hand a warm squeeze as he got to his feet. "Good luck," she whispered.

Mr. Collins smiled at her. "If you don't mind Liz coming along, she's welcome," he said to Jeffrey.

Elizabeth grinned. "I guess you know how to read minds," she teased. It would have been agony waiting for Jeffrey to come back and tell her what happened.

Jim Roberts was waiting for them in the office when they arrived. "I got the message from my math teacher that you wanted to talk to me," he said, looking uncertainly at Elizabeth and Jeffrey.

Mr. Collins nodded, then closed the door of the office. "That's right. I have some good news for both of you. Jeffrey, your photograph won second place in the *News* competition. And"— he turned to Jim with a big smile—"you won first prize, Jim! Your photograph is going to be published on the front page of Friday's paper."

Jim's face turned pale. "My—but wait a second," he said, clearly agitated. "That's impossible. I withdrew my photograph from the competition."

Elizabeth and Jeffrey stared at each other, confused.

"I know," Mr. Collins said, still smiling. "But Shelley came by on Saturday and insisted that we put it back in the running. And," he added, "it won! Congratulations! I can't tell you how proud I am of you both."

Elizabeth couldn't understand the expression on Jim's face. Instead of looking elated, he seemed very distressed.

"What is it, Jim?" she asked, putting her hand on his arm.

"I just can't let that picture be published," he said anxiously. "Mr. Collins—"

But Mr. Collins was busy locating some papers on his desk. "Now, I need you both to sign these release forms from the *News*," he announced. "Jim, your prize will be delivered to you on Friday." He beamed. "Your own video camera, and just in time for you to film the basketball game on Friday."

"Yeah," Jim said, glancing down at the ground. "Right."

Shelley was in the middle of lunch on Thursday when Jim came over to her, a tense expression on his face. "Can I talk to you?" he asked.

Shelley looked across the table at Cathy, whose eyebrows were raised. "Sure," she answered, pointing to the chair next to them.

"Alone," Jim said.

"I was—uh, I was just leaving," Cathy said, scrambling to get all her things together.

"No, stay," Jim said quickly, looking more embarrassed than ever. "I mean . . ."

"I really was about to get going. We have a pep rally this afternoon, and I need to go over a few things with the coach first." Cathy winked at Shelley. "See you at practice," she called over her shoulder as she hurried off.

Shelley looked down at the table. There was no way she could look Jim in the eye.

"Listen," he said anxiously, setting his camera bag down on the table, "I've been trying to find you all day. I even tried to find you yesterday after school, but—"

"I had practice," Shelley said, cutting him off. At once she wanted to kick herself. Why had she been so abrupt?

Her tone seemed to make Jim even more ill at ease. "Oh," he said, fiddling with the shoulder strap of his bag. "Well, the reason I wanted to talk to you was . . ." He frowned, as if he weren't sure quite what to say next. "I mean, I wanted to tell you that it turns out I won the *News* contest."

Shelley stared at him. For a minute she felt overwhelmingly happy for him. "That's fantastic!" she cried.

Jim stared back at her. "I don't understand you," he said. "As far as I knew, I wasn't even *in* that contest anymore. I thought my entry had been taken out. When did you go over to Mr. Collins's house? What did you tell him?"

Shelley's joy subsided. Jim was looking at her suspiciously. "Well," she said carefully, "I thought it over, and it seemed to me that I was really being a poor sport. I mean, you're a really

95

talented photographer. I realized I was being a jerk about it. So I told Mr. Collins to put the picture back in the competition."

Jim bit his lip. "I feel pretty stupid," he said. "I thought you didn't want that picture published. Then I find out that you don't mind after all."

Shelley ran her finger along the edge of her tray. Jim didn't sound particularly happy that she had changed her mind. And she had made a huge sacrifice for him! The thought of that picture appearing in the newspaper was still agonizing for her. But she had tried to ignore her feelings and forget about it, for his sake.

And was he grateful? No! He was acting annoyed that she had been indecisive about the picture at all.

"Well," she said curtly, "I'm sorry if I caused you any trouble, Jim. The fact is, I realized that I was being a poor sport. I talked the whole thing over with Cathy, and she made me see how unfair I was being."

Jim took a deep breath. "So that was what changed your mind, then, thinking that you were being a poor sport."

Shelley nodded. "Anyway," she said, making it sound as though the conversation was more or less over, "I'm glad you won. That's great."

Jim stood, picked up the camera bag, then blurted out, "I feel that you and I—we keep saying the wrong things to each other!" he blurted out.

Shelley knew exactly what he meant. She had been so thrilled to see him when he first came over, and she had hoped there was a chance for them to set everything straight. Instead, they had just made matters worse.

It was obvious that things between her and Jim were never going to be settled. And their relationship was never going to be the same again. It was over, and the sooner she accepted that the better.

"What happened?" Cathy demanded later that afternoon in the gym. She was waiting for Shelley at the pep rally for the girls' basketball team.

"I don't want to talk about it," Shelley said, taking her place on the side of the gym with the rest of the team. "Put it this way," she added. "You should have stuck around. Maybe things would've gone better between Jim and me if you'd been there. We sure manage to mess things up when it's just the two of us!"

"Oh, no," Cathy said sadly. "I was sure you two would straighten everything out. Olivia told me that his photograph won first place in the *News* contest. So wasn't he psyched about that?"

Shelley shook her head. "Not really. He didn't seem very psyched about anything—least of all about seeing me."

Cathy didn't know what to say. "Well, maybe you two just weren't meant to be." She shrugged. "I don't know."

Shelley didn't answer. If that was true, why couldn't she get Jim Roberts out of her mind?

"Watch out!" Amy Sutton snapped at Jessica. The cheerleaders were forming a pyramid at the pep rally, only Amy was so busy trying to be more graceful than Jessica that she kept breaking position.

"Stop it," Jessica hissed back.

"Look, you two," Robin Wilson said to them. "We're working as a team here. Are you trying to kill us all or what?"

Jessica had her eye on Patrick McLean, who was watching the cheerleaders from the bleachers. "See," she whispered to Amy under her breath. "Cut it out, or someone's going to get hurt." Jessica had been horrified when she found out Amy had asked Patrick to come to the pep rally. The humiliation of doing a silly little pyramid in front of him was almost more than she could bear.

"No one's getting hurt, Jessica. It's just that

I'm supposed to be in front and *you're* supposed to be in back," Amy complained.

Robin put her hands on her hips. "I don't know what's going on here. Jessica, you know you're in the back in this formation. Now get into position!"

Jessica glared at Amy. "Fine. You got your way. Now are you happy?" And before Amy could say anything she took her position—completely hidden from Patrick's view—and they completed the cheer.

"He was looking at me! I know he was looking at me!" Amy exclaimed joyfully once they broke up and moved into a long line for the next cheer.

Jessica glowered at her. "Yeah, well, so what," she managed to mutter. "He isn't going to dance with you at the Varsity Club dance tomorrow night. He's going to dance with *me*."

"Want to bet?" Amy challenged her.

Robin put her hands on her hips again. "You guys," she begged, "can't you at least pretend that you're cheerleaders?"

"Yeah," Jessica whispered back to Amy. "What do you want to bet?"

"I bet you"—Amy narrowed her eyes—"a whole outfit at Lisette's that I get him to dance with me tomorrow night before you do."

"You're on," Jessica said grimly, putting her

hand out to shake just as Robin stormed over to tear them apart.

Jessica tried to catch Patrick's eye as she lined up for the next cheer. She was sure she could manage to get him to waltz with her the very first dance.

In fact, she was so sure about it that she almost told Amy to double the bet.

"Do you mean to tell us that your photograph is going to be on the front page of the newspaper tomorrow?" Mrs. Novak exclaimed excitedly.

"Yes," Shelley said quietly, slumping down in a kitchen chair. "That's exactly what I'm telling you. But don't look so happy about it, Mom. Why would you want your giant-sized daughter's picture plastered all over the paper?"

Mrs. Novak shook her head. "I can't believe you, Shelley. It isn't enough that you win every prize and award there is in the world of high school basketball. The fact that a photograph of you won first prize ought to be a hint that you're a beautiful girl. But you still manage to insist that you're a freak." She sighed. "Keep it up, and you just may manage to convince someone you're right. Is that what you want to do?"

Shelley stared at her. Her mother had never

sounded so harsh with her before. "No," she said, her voice trembling.

Her mother wasn't through yet. "Next time I hear you complain about your height I'm marching you right over to the children's hospital so you can see some children born with *real* problems. Then maybe you won't make such a big deal out of being a few inches taller than the other girls in your class."

Shelley felt as if she had been slapped. But she also knew, deep down, that her mother was right. "I'm sorry," she whispered, her face flaming.

Mrs. Novak crossed the room and put her arms around her daughter. "Sweetheart, don't be sorry. Just quit *feeling* sorry—for yourself. Because you're an incredibly lucky girl, with your whole life in front of you."

Shelley nodded, her eyes glistening with unshed tears. "Maybe," she said hopefully, "the picture will look all right."

"Of course it will!" Mrs. Novak said confidently. "And I happen to know someone who's going to drive to every newsstand in town until he finds advance copies of that paper so he can see your picture first thing."

Shelley laughed. "Sounds like Daddy," she said, wiping her eyes.

"That's right," her mother said cheerfully.

"Is there any way I can convince you to stay up late enough tonight to look at the picture with us?"

"I can't, Mom. I promised the coach that I'd be in bed by ten o'clock at the very latest. If we don't all get a good night's sleep, we risk throwing away the game tomorrow. And besides, tomorrow's going to be a really big day."

"That's right," her mother mused. "You've got the game, then the dance."

And Jim's picture of me in the newspaper, Shelley thought wistfully.

She had a sudden image of dancing with Jim that made her heart beat more quickly. If only she hadn't blown it by being too defensive—too quick to blame him for something that really wasn't his fault.

Well, all she could do was give the game tomorrow her all. Maybe one day she and Jim could be friends again. And for the time being, her mother was right. She needed to stop feeling sorry for herself and count her blessings.

Still, a tiny little part of her could feel sorry about Jim Roberts. And that tiny little part just couldn't stop thinking about him.

Ten

"Have you seen today's copy of the *News*?" Amy Sutton demanded, flinging the paper across the table at Jessica. It was Friday during lunchtime, and a large group had gathered at one of the tables. Everyone was busy talking about the basketball game and the dance afterward at the hotel, but Amy's question silenced the whole table.

"Let me see!" Jessica cried, lunging for the paper.

But Lila and Cara had gotten to it first. "Let *me* see," Lila cried. The bottom part of the paper tore, and Jessica snatched the top part free.

"I can't believe it!" she exclaimed, staring. "It's Shelley Novak!"

"Why does *she* get her picture in the paper?" Lila demanded.

Cara was staring at the photograph over Jessica's shoulder. "Wow," she said. "Shelley looks fantastic!"

"She sure does," Jessica agreed. "Boy, I'd kill to have legs that long."

Amy raised her eyebrows. "Too bad you don't," she said to Jessica. "Too bad you're so much *shorter* than Pat McLean."

"Since when do you call him Pat?" Jessica shrieked.

"Stop it, you two," Lila said. "We're sick and tired of hearing you squabble over poor Patrick McLean. For all either of you know, he could be married." She turned back to Shelley's photograph and examined it with interest. "So Jim Roberts won the competition," she mused. "This is a gorgeous photograph."

Jessica, still stricken by the thought that Patrick could be married or have a girlfriend, turned back to look at Shelley's photograph. It really was fabulous. Shelley seemed to be suspended in midair, and her body was so graceful that she almost looked like a dancer. The photograph was titled "Poetry in Motion," and a brief interview with Jim had been printed just below it on the page.

"Shelley's so lucky," Cara said, studying the picture. "Imagine having your picture on the

104

front page of the paper the day of the big basketball playoff game! She must be ecstatic!"

"Yeah, and it's such a flattering picture, too," Amy said.

Jessica gave her an annoyed look. "You are the nastiest person alive, Amy. You're probably just jealous as usual, because you know if Shelley Novak had more confidence, she could be a model."

"I'll bet Shelley's going out of her mind with excitement," Cara added. "I'm going to go find her and tell her how great I think she looks."

"Wow," Cathy said, unfolding the paper and staring at Shelley's photograph, her eyes wide. "This is fantastic, Shel!"

Shelley was eating her sandwich, and she didn't bother to look up. "I haven't seen it yet," she said matter-of-factly. "And I don't really want to, either."

Cathy shook her head in disbelief. "You haven't looked at a picture of yourself that thousands of other people have seen? Are you nuts?"

"Maybe. But I'm trying to get psyched up for the game today," Shelley said calmly. "I don't feel like looking at the picture now. Do you mind?"

"Put it this way," Cathy said. "If someone took

a picture of me that made me look that good, *I'd* want to look at it."

Just then Cara Walker walked up and dragged a chair over to their table. "Shelley, I can't even believe how wonderful you look in this photograph," she said enthusiastically, sitting down and putting the paper on the table.

Before Shelley could answer, a whole gang of kids had descended on her. Lila, Winston Egbert, Jessica, and all of them wanted to tell her how great she looked in the picture. Shelley just stared at them. She still hadn't looked at the photograph.

"Shelley's a little shy about the whole thing," Cathy explained when it became obvious her friend was too tongue-tied to respond.

"You should think about becoming a fashion model, Shelley," Lila said. "You know, I've thought about modeling myself, but I'm just not tall enough." The comment provoked a few barely suppressed snickers from Jessica and Amy, who knew Lila's attempt to become a model had ended in complete disaster.

But Lila's suggestion was lost in the jumble of excited comments from the crowd. Everyone wanted to know if Shelley had posed for Jim or if he had only taken candids and if the two of them were good friends and whether Shelley was always this photogenic. She couldn't believe her ears. By the time the din had subsided and people had drifted away again, she couldn't resist picking up Cathy's copy of the paper.

She unfolded it slowly and stared at the photograph. For a brief moment the old panic came over her, and she saw herself as a girl who was too tall for everything—even basketball. But the next minute a very different emotion overcame her as she studied the picture.

She could see what they meant. It *was* beautiful.

Correction, Shelley thought, *she* was beautiful.

She had never been able to think that about herself. Jim had caught her in so graceful a leap that she appeared to be floating. She looked strong, resilient, and in control. "Poetry in Motion" she read below the picture. That was when her eyes flooded with tears.

"I've got to get another carton of milk," Cathy said quietly, seeming to guess that Shelley needed to be alone then. Shelley nodded, barely noticing when her friend left. She was reading the interview with Jim.

The interviewer had asked Jim what his feelings were regarding the photo. "I was very lucky to have Shelley for a subject," Jim answered. "Her motions are so beautiful. I wanted to capture some of what I'd guessed she feels for her sport—some of the intensity, some of the grace. I fell in love with this picture, and even though my subject was camera-shy, I couldn't bring myself to destroy it. It was just too precious to me."

Shelley felt a tear trickle down her cheek. Instead of feeling embarrassed or angry that Jim had said something so personal, she felt incredibly moved. What came across in the interview was that he had a special feeling for her. Or at least, he had *had* that feeling before they both destroyed it through their stupid misunderstanding.

Shelley turned back to the photograph and studied it, fascinated. *Intensity* and *grace*, those were the words Jim had chosen. And those words seemed to capture what came across in the picture. For all these years Shelley had been unable to comprehend that anyone could see her as graceful. Intense, maybe. Graceful, never. Not until today.

She jumped to her feet. Suddenly Shelley wanted more than anything in the entire world to find Jim Roberts and tell him how much she liked the picture. *And* how much she liked him.

"Go, Sweet Valley! Sweet Valley, go!" the cheerleaders screamed. It was four-thirty, and the fourth game in the playoffs between Sweet Valley and Emerson was in the second quarter.

Emerson was leading by four points, and it looked as if the game would be a tough one.

"Pass it, Shel!" Cathy called out.

Shelley tried to pass her teammate the ball, but she stumbled, sending the ball right into the hands of the Emerson forward. *What a klutz*, Shelley scolded herself, running up the court with her head down.

It wasn't her game, and she knew why. All afternoon she had tried to find Jim. Not just to tell him about his picture, either. Shelley had realized the truth the minute she read that interview. She was in love with Jim Roberts. Really in love, not a stupid crush like the one she'd had on Greg Hilliard. And she wanted desperately to make things work out between them.

But she hadn't been able to find him. She had looked everywhere—in the lunchroom, in the darkroom, in the student lounge. No Jim. By the time the game started, Shelley was already feeling beaten. She had felt so dazzling when she first saw the photograph of herself. Now it was as if her feet were made out of lead.

Jim wasn't in his usual place on the sidelines, either. Shelley kept checking the stands for him, but he was nowhere to be seen.

"Come on, Shelley! What's wrong with you?"

Cathy cried, watching with alarm as her friend dropped yet another pass.

"I'm sorry. I'm just too tense," Shelley muttered, running over to the sidelines to wipe her face on a towel when the coach called a time-out.

She could barely listen to his words of encouragement as he faced the team. Whether he said it or not, she knew it was her fault they were losing. She was playing like a beginner instead of an award-winner. She didn't deserve anyone's praise for her performance in this game.

"Tighten up on defense. Cathy, watch the center—she's giving us a lot of problems. Shelley" —the coach eyed her thoughtfully—"try to lighten up a little. Don't play like this is the last game in the world. Try to have fun out there."

Shelley nodded woodenly. How could she have fun when all she could think about was the disaster with Jim? That had been all her fault, too.

By the halftime break Sweet Valley High and Emerson were tied 70–70. If Sweet Valley could pull ahead and win, they would win the playoffs and go on to the state competition.

But that was *if* they won, Shelley thought despairingly. She didn't know about the others, but she felt like a wreck, as if every bit of energy had been squeezed out of her already.

Cathy nudged her in the ribs as they sat

down for the break. "I just saw a friend of yours show up." She nodded toward the bleachers.

Jim had come to the game! Shelley thought. She narrowed her eyes, squinting up at the bleachers, watching him climb up to an empty space. As he sat down she caught a glimpse of his camera on a strap around his neck.

Shelley ran over to Coach Tilman's chair on the sideline. There was enough time left before the third quarter to do something to let Jim know how she felt about him. "Can I borrow a piece of paper and a pencil? I have to send someone a note," she explained, trying to keep the urgency out of her voice. "Please?"

The coach looked at her disapprovingly. Shelley knew it was bad sportsmanship to concentrate on anything but the game, but she had to send Jim a note. Until she did, until she saw his reaction, she just couldn't put her heart into the game.

"OK, but make it quick," Coach Tilman said, handing her his clipboard and a pencil.

Hastily she scribbled the following message:

Thank you for the most beautiful picture in the world. You said in the interview you couldn't throw it out because you'd fallen in love with it. That's exactly how I feel about *you*. Is there any way in the world we can make up? I want to take you to the dance with me tonight.

She hesitated for a minute. Then she signed it, "Poetry in Motion."

She looked around for someone to deliver the note. Maria Santelli, one of the cheerleaders, was right near Shelley, tying the shoelace on her tennis shoe. "Maria, would you do me a huge favor and run this note up to Jim Roberts?" Shelley asked. She pointed out the place where he was sitting.

Maria looked confused, but she nodded. "Sure, Shelley," she said. "By the way, that was a great picture of you in the paper today."

"Thanks," Shelley said. Her stomach was churning as she watched the petite brunette scramble up the bleachers. There . . . she had almost reached Jim . . . she was giving him the note.

Shelley felt her face burn as Jim looked curiously from Maria down to the spot on the floor where Shelley was standing. Then Maria started to climb down again, and Jim unfolded the note.

To Shelley it seemed forever before Jim got to his feet and searched for her. He had such a strange look on his face. Was he glad, or was he upset with her? Shelley couldn't tell.

A minute later their eyes met, and Shelley knew the answer. An enormous smile covered Jim's face, and she knew her own smile mirrored his.

He picked up his camera with a quizzical look, and Shelley nodded, still smiling. She knew she could play the second half of the game now—and she knew she could win it for Sweet Valley. With Jim watching her, she could do anything—even if he took a thousand pictures of her!

Eleven

The second half of the basketball game seemed to go by in a flash. Shelley knew she had never played so well before. Every pass flew into her fingers; every shot she made went through the hoop smoothly, never touching the rim. By the end of the fourth quarter, Sweet Valley was beating Emerson, 108–80, and Shelley had set a school record for scoring the most baskets in a single game.

But even more important, she knew Jim was rooting for her. When she heard the crowd roar with applause, she knew he was out there cheering her on.

The clock wound down to the final seconds, and Shelley had the ball.

"Novak! Novak!" the crowd screamed as they got to their feet. Shelley charged up the court with the ball to dunk Sweet Valley's final basket. Suddenly it was over, and Sweet Valley had won the girls' league playoffs, 110–80, three games to one!

The next thing Shelley knew, her teammates were sweeping her up on their shoulders, yelling her name in unison, and carrying her along toward the crowd of students, reporters, and photographers bearing down on them. Shelley felt dozens of hands supporting her, and her heart was pounding wildly. It had been the best game of her life.

Reporters from the *News* were pressing in all around the team to ask her questions. "Did you feel you had the game the whole time, or were you nervous at the end of the half?" "How does it feel to have scored so many baskets?" "What college are you thinking of going to?"

But Shelley was barely paying attention to the crowd. Her eyes were scanning the throng of people for Jim. At last she saw him hurrying toward her, and her face lit up.

"Can we get a picture of you?" the *News* photographer asked Shelley.

She laughed. "Actually, there's someone here who's kind of—well, I'd really like it if *he'd* take my picture and let you use it." She pointed to Jim.

The *News* photographer looked at Jim, puzzled. "Say, aren't you the guy who just won the contest we sponsored?"

Jim nodded, but he kept staring at Shelley.

"Well, then, be my guest," the photographer said with a smile.

Shelley smiled straight at Jim. She was sure he would take wonderful pictures of her and the team. In fact, she couldn't believe she had ever doubted him. "OK, cameraman," she said, "start shooting!"

A crowd was still hanging around the girls' team fifteen minutes later. The coach was talking about the team's chances in the state championship, the cheerleaders were congratulating the players, and a number of friends and fans were still standing around, talking excitedly about the game. Shelley had a towel around her neck and was deep in conversation with Cathy, Jim, and several friends when Greg Hilliard pushed his way through the crowd.

"Shelley, let me give you a hug," he said exuberantly.

Shelley gave him a brief smile. Greg hadn't had much time for her before she won the game for the team. Now he was acting as if they were incredibly close. But before she could say a word, Greg had engulfed her in a huge embrace. It was a little more affectionate than Shelley had expected, and she could see an anxious expression cross Jim's face.

"You were terrific out there, Shel. Really terrific," Greg continued. He kept his arm around her while he talked. "And you know something? I *love* that photograph of you in the newspaper. You look fantastic, you know that?"

"Thanks," Shelley said, trying to edge away from him a little. "Actually, Jim took it." She signaled to Jim, who was looking increasingly uncomfortable.

"No kidding?" Greg didn't seem to care. "Well, that's great. But the point is, you really look terrific in that picture, Shelley. Like, I don't know, some kind of actress or a dancer or something. So speaking of dancing . . ."

Shelley pulled herself free from Greg. She really didn't like the way he was acting—as if he owned her.

"Speaking of dancing," Greg continued, not seeming to mind that the whole crowd around them had hushed to listen, "what do you think about going to the dance with me tonight, after all?"

Shelley couldn't believe her ears. Greg? Asking her to the dance? After what he said to her when she'd asked him?

"No, thanks," she told him. Her voice sounded a little colder than she had intended, and she added quickly, smiling at Jim, "I already have a date."

It gave her a real jolt of pleasure to take Jim's hand and slip off through the crowd with him, leaving Greg staring after her as if he didn't know what had hit him!

"I owe you a huge apology," Shelley said to Jim, her eyes fixed steadily on his. Jim had offered her a ride home from the game, but on the way they had stopped at the beach to take a walk. It was late in the day and the beach was almost deserted, so they had complete privacy. "I made much too big a deal out of having my picture taken. It's just that I've always had such a problem with self-esteem that I couldn't believe anyone would want a picture of me. Does that make sense?"

Jim nodded. "It does. I mean, it's hard for me to imagine it, given how pretty you are. But, yes, it makes sense. And I think I'm the one who owes you an apology. I should've respected your feelings and known better than to enter that contest. Or I could have at least submitted a different picture. It was just—" He looked at her intently. "It was just that I really did fall in love with that picture. It caught so much of you. I wanted to share it with the world."

Shelley put her hand on his arm. "So," she said softly, "you fell in love—with that picture?"

Jim's eyes were filled with emotion as he gently lifted her chin with his finger and stared searchingly into her eyes. "Not just with the picture," he whispered. He wrapped his arms around her and pulled her close to him.

The next minute they were clinging to each other and kissing, finally able to express how they felt.

"So," Elizabeth said to Jeffrey, turning to him with a smile. It was early Friday evening, and they were sitting in the Wakefields' driveway in Jeffrey's car. "How does it feel to be a major prize-winning photographer? Still willing to show up at the dance with me tonight?"

"Oh," Jeffrey said, leaning over to give her a kiss, "I think I could be persuaded." He was thoughtful for a minute. "You know, the more of Jim's stuff I see, the more I think he's going to be a first-rate photographer one day."

"I know." Elizabeth nodded. "I'm glad his picture got published. It's really going to boost his confidence."

"I heard a *News* photographer say he thought they might be able to give Jim some free-lance work doing photography for the paper. This could really be the start of something big for him."

Elizabeth looked at Jeffrey thoughtfully. "No hard feelings about it? You're not upset you didn't come in first?"

Jeffrey shook his head. "Absolutely not. I feel lucky to gave gotten an award at all. Jim's in a different league—he's naturally talented. Yet he works so hard at it, too."

"One of the reasons I happen to be so crazy about you, Jeffrey French, is that you're unbelievably grown-up about stuff like this," Elizabeth admitted.

"Does that mean you're going to dance with me tonight? Or am I going to have to fend off the crowds of eligible young bachelors?"

Elizabeth giggled. Then she glanced at her watch and let out a little shriek. "If you're going to dance with a girl wearing anything other than these old jeans, I'd better get out of this car right now and start getting ready!" She jumped out of the car and leaned through the open window to give Jeffrey another kiss. "See you soon."

A few minutes after Jeffrey pulled out of the drive, Elizabeth ran upstairs and knocked on the door to the bathroom that separated her bedroom from her sister's.

"Jess? Can you hear me?"

After a long pause the door opened and steam billowed out. Jessica, her body wrapped in one towel and her hair wrapped in another, stared at her twin from behind a cosmetic face mask the color of cucumbers. "Hi," she said, a bottle of nail polish in one hand and an emery board in the other.

"Jess, I need to take a shower," Elizabeth moaned, staring past her sister into the impenetrable steam. "What's going on in here? You're going to melt the wallpaper off the walls."

"I was steaming my pores open," Jessica said calmly. "I'll be out in about fifteen minutes—I promise. I just have to soak my fingers before I do my nails."

"I'm going to soak more than your fingers if you don't let me in sooner than that," Elizabeth threatened. She knew by "Jessica time" that fifteen minutes would be more like an hour, and she really did need to get ready.

"OK," Jessica said, unperturbed. "Hey, Liz, you want to see the dress I'm wearing tonight?" She padded out of the bathroom, her wet feet making marks on the carpeting, and Elizabeth followed her.

Elizabeth whistled when she saw the dress spread out on Jessica's bed. It was the very latest fashion, a strapless dress with a puffy

121

skirt in a beautiful shade of lilac. "Where'd you get the money for that?"

"Oh," Jessica said mildly, "I just used some of the money in my savings account. Well, most of it, I guess. Amy and I have a bet that I know I can win, and she's going to owe me the cost of the dress."

Elizabeth narrowed her eyes. "You're *that* sure you can win? What's the bet about?"

Jessica started wiping the mask off with a tissue. "Well, Patrick McLean's coming to the dance tonight. The principal invited him. Amy's got the absurd idea that she can get him to dance with her tonight before I can." Jessica wiped another streak of face mask off. "It's perfectly obvious he doesn't like her. I mean, just the one time he danced with me in class I could tell how he *really* felt. It's just fate, Liz. Total fate. He's the guy for me, I can tell."

"Right," Elizabeth said with a chuckle. She had heard her twin say the same thing about so many guys by now that she couldn't even bring herself to argue with her. "So you bet Amy that you can get Patrick to dance with you before she can?"

Jessica nodded. "It's a sure bet. The only problem is, I'll have to get to the dance pretty early. I hate to be unfashionably on time, but it would be just like Amy to pull something like getting there before me and forcing him to dance with her first."

Elizabeth picked up the price tag, which was still dangling from the dress. "Well, I hope you win, Jess. Otherwise, this could be the greatest financial setback since the stock market crash."

"How could I possibly not win the bet?"

Elizabeth shrugged. It was true that when her sister wanted something this badly, she usually got it. "You're sure Patrick's coming to this dance?"

"Positive. He told us during our last lesson. Weren't you there? We were learning the cha-cha." Jessica did a few steps to show Elizabeth, who cracked up at the sight of her towel-clad twin, with half of her face still covered by the mask, cha-cha-cha-ing in her bedroom.

"I missed that class. I was out with Jeffrey," Elizabeth admitted. "Well, good luck, Jess. I'm going to see if I can survive the steam you left in the bathroom and get ready for the dance myself."

"Wait!" Jessica shrieked. "I left all my nail stuff in there." She raced into the bathroom, emerging a minute later with all her manicure supplies.

Elizabeth wiped off the mirror in the bathroom and opened the window to get rid of some of the steam. "You know," she said conversationally, "this should be a pretty big night for Shelley Novak. Do you think she's going to get some kind of special award from the Varsity Club?"

"I don't know. Did you see Jim's picture of her in the paper today? She looked great." Jessica dashed cold water on her face to get rid of the rest of the mask. "Boy, I wouldn't mind having a boyfriend like Jim Roberts. Imagine getting your picture in the paper all the time." Her eyes shone. "Maybe after Patrick and I get engaged, we can tour all over, doing the tango and the cha-cha, and our picture will be plastered all over the place." She sighed. "Who knows? We might even hire Jim to be our personal photographer."

Elizabeth groaned. "You're counting on an awful lot," she commented.

Jessica was too busy daydreaming to respond. She almost wished she had charged a pair of shoes at Lisette's to match her dress. As it was, she was letting Amy off too easy!

Twelve

Shelley took a deep breath, then stepped back and looked at herself in the mirror. She couldn't believe her eyes.

"You look beautiful," her mother whispered.

Shelley couldn't stop staring at herself. For the first time in her life, she liked what she saw.

When she had gotten home from the basketball game, her mother had surprised her with a big box from a store Shelley had never heard of before. Inside was the most gorgeous dress Shelley had ever seen. It fitted her perfectly. It was much sleeker and more sophisticated than anything Shelley had ever worn. It was made of a light gray silk fabric that gleamed like silver, with off-the-shoulder sleeves and a soft skirt that made her want to dance right then and there. That wasn't all. Her mother had spent ages with Shelley, putting mousse on her hair and styling it, then applying makeup to dramatize her large gray eyes. She really did look like a model when she was ready.

"You know," her mother added, admiring the dress, "I'm going to say something that may surprise you. But the reason you look beautiful has nothing to do with the new dress and the makeup. I don't know what happened to you this week, but you're like a whole new person, Shelley. I've never seen you hold your head so high. You look positively regal."

Shelley gave her a hug. "Oh, Mom," she said. She knew what had changed. It was only partly the fact that she had met someone she really cared about—and had a genuine boyfriend instead of an impossible, silly crush on Greg Hilliard. It had more to do with the fact she had learned, finally, to have some confidence in herself. She didn't hate being tall anymore. She was different from other girls, sure, but that didn't mean there was anything wrong with her.

The door bell rang, and Shelley's mother got to her feet. "That must be Jim," she said. "Should I go downstairs and tell him you're nearly ready?"

Shelley nodded, her eyes shining. And when

her mother left the room, she spun around in a circle so that she could see the soft gray dress twirl around her legs. She couldn't wait to dance in Jim's arms! And she knew that this time she wasn't going to feel like a klutz.

The Varsity Club dance was being held in a ballroom at the new Royal Hotel in downtown Sweet Valley. Though the purpose of the dance was to honor athletes, the whole school had been invited, and it looked as though there would be a big turnout. Jessica hated to leave her post on the front steps of the hotel, where she had been watching everyone arrive. There was nothing Jessica loved more than seeing who came with whom, who had new dresses, who looked good and who didn't. But, of course, the main point of her post on the steps was to watch out for Patrick—and for Amy.

The dance officially began at eight o'clock. By eight-fifteen Patrick hadn't arrived. Jessica was craning her neck, trying to get a glimpse of him, when she saw something that made her heart stand still.

At first she couldn't believe her eyes. She thought she must be seeing things, and she actually rubbed her eyes and blinked twice.

But there was Amy Sutton, bouncing up the

steps to the hotel, her blond hair shining, her eyes bright. That wasn't what was making Jessica so crazy, though. Amy always looked good.

What she was staring at was Amy's dress: strapless, lilac, with a puffy skirt: the *exact* same dress Jessica was wearing!

Jessica's eyes widened with horror. Amy hadn't seen her yet. She was too busy skipping lightly up the steps in a pair of silvery sandals that Jessica had to admit looked even better with the dress than the cream-colored pumps she herself was wearing. Then Amy stopped short, and all the happiness vanished from her face. Her mouth dropped open in surprise.

"Just what do you think you're doing?" Jessica demanded harshly.

Lila Fowler was climbing up the steps with her date, and she stopped to gaze at Amy and Jessica with amused interest. "Jessica, I thought you had enough of that twin stuff with your own sister," she commented dryly.

"Ha, ha, very funny, Lila," Jessica said.

"Jessica Wakefield, get out of that dress right now!" Amy practically shouted.

"What do you mean, get out of it? What am I supposed to do, go to the dance naked? Besides, why should *I* get out of it? It's *my* dress," Jessica said coldly. "I happen to have bought mine on Tuesday."

"So what?" Amy cried. "Jessica, there's no way we're going into that ballroom wearing the identical dress. I'd rather die."

"So die," Jessica said furiously.

Amy was about to say the same thing to Jessica when her gray eyes flew open even wider. "Jess, look," she whispered, staring down the stairs as a white limousine pulled up. Patrick McLean was getting out of the backseat. "He looks *so* gorgeous," Amy crooned, her anger and humiliation apparently forgotten as she stared at the handsome young man. Patrick looked even more striking than usual in a simple black tuxedo. He really did look like a movie star.

Jessica stared at him, too. But her pleasure at seeing Patrick was replaced by shock as she watched him turn back to the limousine, extend his hand, and help someone out.

"Oh, no," Amy moaned. "He's got a *date*!"

And not just any date. The woman who got out of the limo was startlingly beautiful. She looked a little older than Patrick, maybe twenty-four or so, and she was wearing a designer dress, all glitter, and a real diamond necklace!

"You're not going to find anyone here with *her* dress," Amy said. The two girls stood staring down at Patrick and his date, their faces fixed in identical expressions of dejection. When Patrick climbed the stairs, he smiled at them.

"You two look adorable," he said.

His date's eyes flicked over their dresses, her eyebrows raised. Jessica felt ready to die with humiliation. She couldn't bear it for another second.

"Well, I guess we both messed up," Amy said after Patrick and his date had entered the main door of the hotel.

Jessica didn't feel ready to forgive her yet. "Maybe," she said frostily.

"Jess, don't you see just the tiniest bit of humor in this whole thing?" Amy said, beginning to giggle.

Jessica tossed her head back, ready to make a mean retort. But she couldn't help giggling a little bit, too. They really did look ridiculous together.

And under the circumstances, what could they possibly do but laugh?

After an hour of dancing, white-haired Coach Schultz, the head coach at Sweet Valley High, tapped a spoon against his wineglass to signal that the awards ceremony would begin. The crowd fell silent as they listened to the coach's brief speech. He thanked them all for coming and for their support of the athletic program at Sweet Valley High. Then he read a long list of the athletes who had earned letters that year, and he asked everyone for a round of applause.

Shelley was standing right next to Jim on the dance floor, enjoying herself immensely. The dance had been even more fun so far than she could ever have imagined. Seeing Greg with Carol no longer bothered her. In fact, she hoped they were as happy as she and Jim were.

"Now, there's one very special part of our program tonight," Coach Schultz continued. "This year we are lucky to be able to give a very special award. Our benefactors have established a trust fund for one star athlete, the money to be used as funds for college."

The whole ballroom was very still as everyone stared at each other. No one had expected this to happen. Shelley felt her mouth go dry.

"This year we had a number of exceptional athletes, and it was extremely difficult to decide among them. But I think that, after this afternoon, you'll all agree with our decision. I'd like you all to join me in congratulating Shelley Novak as our very first Varsity Club Athlete of the Year!"

The whole ballroom erupted into wild applause. Shelley was so stunned, she couldn't move. "Shel," Jim whispered, squeezing her shoulder. "You need to go up there!"

The applause grew deafening as Shelley climbed up the stairs to take the certificate and the medal Mr. Townsend handed her. In her wildest dreams she couldn't have imagined this. A five-thousand-dollar college scholarship!

Shelley's eyes filled with tears as she looked out over the audience. Then she singled out Jim's face, and the tears spilled over. She was certain she had never known before what it felt like to be really happy. Next to Jim, she saw Cathy lift her right arm and make a fist, giving her the victory signal. And without hesitation, Shelley raised her arm and gave her the signal right back.

Patrick McLean stood in the center of the ballroom and clapped his hands to get everyone's attention. "This is a surprise," he announced, giving them all a big smile. "But my date, Ellen, has given me a wonderful idea."

Amy and Jessica rolled their eyes at each other in disgust.

"We're going to have a dance contest. The dance will be a waltz. The couple who wins will get a free set of lessons at the McLean Studio when it opens next month in Sweet Valley."

Everyone applauded, and the band hired by the Varsity Club began playing a lovely Viennese waltz as the couples who knew how to waltz came forward.

"Should we try?" Jim asked Shelley with a smile.

"Why not?" she said, giving him her hand. "We're on a roll."

Only ten couples were competing. Shelley noticed Greg and Carol out on the floor. Kurt Campbell and Jessica waltzed right next to Amy Sutton and Bruce Patman, and Shelley almost started to laugh when she saw the girls were wearing the same dresses. Something told her they hadn't planned that. Elizabeth and Jeffrey, Lila and her date, and several couples from the senior and sophomore classes whom Shelley didn't know were also in the contest. After the first movement of the waltz, Patrick and his date selected four couples to continue: Greg and Carol, Jessica and Kurt, Amy and Bruce, and Shelley and Jim!

"I can't believe it," Jim said with a grin. "How come I'm not stepping on your feet this time?"

Shelley smiled deep into his eyes. *For the same reason I feel graceful in your arms*, she thought. *Because . . .*

"Because you make me feel so happy that everything's possible when we're together," he whispered.

Shelley listened to the music and just enjoyed

being in Jim's arms for the next few minutes. She wasn't really aware of what was going on around her, though she did hear Jessica and Amy shriek as they collided, and heard uproarious laughter from the crowd as the two girls and their partners were eliminated. She couldn't believe it, though, when the second movement ended and Patrick announced that the contest was down to two couples: Greg and Carol, and Shelley and Jim.

"Good luck, Novak," Greg said, punching her lightly on the arm.

Shelley smiled. Never in a million years could she have guessed this would happen. But here she was, dancing in the arms of a guy she was in love with, competing for first place in a *dance* contest against Greg!

She closed her eyes, trying to feel that her movements were part of the music. The next thing she knew, the applause was overwhelming, and Patrick had declared Shelley and Jim the winners.

They just stood there grinning at each other when the lights came up. They knew they had won, all right. And it had nothing to do with winning the photography competition or the waltz contest or the Athlete of the Year Award. It had to do with finding each other. That made them the biggest winners of all.

And right there, in front of everyone, Jim took Shelley in his arms and kissed her so tenderly that she thought she must be dreaming. But it was real—and Jim was real. And they had started a relationship that Shelley hoped would never end.

"You know," Jessica said to Amy, "if I were you, I wouldn't still be holding a grudge."

"Well, you aren't me," Amy snapped. It was Monday, and the two girls were in chemistry lab, trying to finish their experiment. "How am I ever going to pay my mom back for that stupid dress?" Amy demanded.

Jessica shrugged. "Got me. Maybe we can sell them to a couple of girls going to a costume party." She giggled. "As Tweedledum and Tweedledee."

"I don't think it's very funny," Amy said morosely. "I wish Patrick McLean had never showed up with those stupid dance lessons of his."

Mr. Russo suddenly appeared at Amy's elbow and frowned at the two girls. "You know, I'm going to have to ask you two to stay late today to catch up on this project. This talking in class isn't helping your grades, either." He cleared his throat. "I'm afraid that in your cases, the optional science trip to Anacapa Island next Sunday is *not* going to be an option."

Jessica raised her eyebrows. "What do you mean?" she asked.

"I mean, you both need the extra-credit points pretty badly." Mr. Russo looked serious. "I'm going to give the whole class more details about the trip later. But I suggest you two consider it mandatory."

"Now look what you've done," Jessica whispered to Amy once Mr. Russo had stepped away to inspect someone else's project.

Amy made a face. "Maybe we can throw our dresses over the side of the boat," she whispered back. "That way we'll never have to see them again!"

Mr. Russo waited till five minutes before the bell to remind everyone that an optional science field trip would take place on Sunday. A group of students and teachers would take a boat out to Anacapa Island to study marine life and to do some ecological checks on water samples. "Any volunteers should sign up right after class," he added, looking meaningfully at Jessica and Amy.

Jessica groaned. The last thing she wanted to do was crawl around looking at fish on Anacapa

Island. But thanks to Amy, it looked like she was stuck.

"I hope good people end up going," she said quietly to her friend.

Amy rolled her eyes. "Why would anyone worthwhile want to fool around with snails and fish eggs on a weekend? Forget it, Jess. I'm going to find some way to get out of this no matter what!"

Jessica just laughed. "Yeah, well, good luck, Amy!"

Who could tell? Maybe a field trip to Anacapa Island would end up being kind of fun—especially if someone interesting, someone *male*, would be on board to divert her from Mr. Russo and the fish!

Will the science field trip go according to Jessica's plans? Find out in Sweet Valley High #56, **LOST AT SEA.**